"I'll help your sister... on one condition."

Gregg's lips trailed over Tanis's warm cheeks as he continued, "You must let the world know you're my woman."

"But that's blackmail!" Tanis cried. "I've never been any man's woman! It's unethical."

Tanis started to leave, but he caught her arms and pulled her back to face him. "I want an answer," he said. Their bodies were touching again, and she gazed up into his eyes, surprised at the desire gleaming back at her.

"No love?" she murmured. "You want me to be your woman without love?"

"Give me one good reason for loving you," Gregg said smoothly.

Because I love you... Tanis wanted to say it, but of course she didn't. Just because she was in love with Gregg didn't mean he loved her—or ever would.

LILIAN PEAKE

gregg barratt's woman

Harlequin Books

TORONTO • LONDON • LOS ANGELES • AMSTERDAM
SYDNEY • HAMBURG • PARIS • STOCKHOLM • ATHENS • TOKYO

Harlequin Presents edition published April 1981
ISBN 0-373-10424-3

Original hardcover edition published in 1981
by Mills & Boon Limited

CHAPTER ONE

IF IT HAD NOT BEEN for her friend's persuasion to stay and keep her company, Tanis would have given up long ago and gone home.

"You can't leave me alone here at the roadside," Edna insisted, pulling Tanis nearer as they huddled together under the umbrella. "It was only when I told my father you were coming that he let me come today."

Tanis sighed and answered, "Just half an hour longer, then I really will have to go over there and ask Mrs. Beasley to come and collect me."

"Good," said Edna. "That's only a quarter of an hour to when my father's coming for me—and what's left of the flowers." She indicated the small covered table on which flowers were arranged in buckets, ready-made into bouquets for people to buy and take home or to give to patients at a nearby hospital.

"You're lucky," Tanis remarked, staring gloomily along the road. "At least you've sold a few bunches of flowers. I haven't sold a single one of Cassandra's paintings."

"Look how wet they're getting," Edna commiserated. "Although I told my father you were coming, I did wonder whether you would in this weather."

"I had to take a chance. We need every bit of money we can get."

"How is Cassie?" Edna asked.

"In herself, she's fine. It's just her legs...." Her voice trailed off into a silence filled by the constant pat-

ter of rain and the rushing noise of speeding car wheels
on the road's wet surface.

"How far have you got toward your target for her
treatment?" Edna asked.

"About a quarter of the way. And that's taken much
longer than we estimated."

There was the hiss of tires on the wet surface of the
road. A long, low car slid to a halt on the shoulder just
past the two staring girls. Tanis's hands clenched into
fists. "He wants a rest," she intoned, "a drink of coffee, or a look at a map." Her eyes closed tightly. "He's
not, repeat, *not* interested in the paintings. A man driving a car that big never buys pictures exhibited at a roadside stand. He goes to famous galleries in London...."

"He's getting out," Edna reported, whispering.
"He's walking over to the paintings." Tanis covered her
ears, but Edna tugged one of her hands away. "Listen,
silly. He's bending down, inspecting them—standing
back and staring. He's getting wet, but he doesn't seem
to be worried."

"In about two minutes from now," Tanis stated
resignedly, "he'll be back in his car and away."

"Wrong," Edna whispered excitedly. "He's coming
this way."

Tanis's eyes opened and gazed around while her body
remained huddled under the umbrella. She saw a tall
brown-haired man in a green water-repellent zippered
jacket, his hands slipped into the pockets of his dark,
dampened slacks. He looked first at Edna, then at
Tanis, whose immediate reaction was to look away.

Right the first time, she told herself. Not the kind to
buy; not with his detached, exclusive air, his penetrating
eyes and his heart-tipping looks.

"Which of you do I ask about those pictures?" His
voice was deep, his question containing a hint of amusement. If he was mocking her sister's work, Tanis
thought, then he could go on his way like all the others.

It seemed, however, that it was not the paintings that had caused the faint smile. "You need a larger umbrella," he commented. "You're getting wet."

Tanis forced a laugh. She supposed it was kind of him to be "just looking" in this weather. "It would take a lot worse than this to dampen our enthusiasm."

The man's eyebrows rose and fell. The action was a comment in itself. Had she put him off by appearing too eager, Tanis wondered. Or was she frightening him away by her less than positive sales technique?

"Are they your paintings?" the man asked Tanis. Looking up at him, she saw the intriguing amber color of his eyes.

"No, my sister's."

His glance moved to Edna, who shook her head.

"My sister's at home," Tanis explained hurriedly. "Edna's my friend. She's in charge of the flowers. There's—there's a hospital not far away."

The man nodded. "I know. The pictures—can you give me an idea of their cost?"

"Oh, yes." Tanis's heartbeats started to quicken. Was this leading to a sale, after all? Just one, just the sale of a miniature would give Cassandra encouragement. Turning up her jacket collar, she moved quickly across to the railings to which the pictures were fixed. The local council had given her permission to display them there.

Tanis pointed to the price list. "It's covered in protective film," she explained, "like the paintings. The rain shouldn't affect them. Anyway, they're all in oils. I left the watercolors at home."

"Very wise," the man remarked. As Tanis turned to go, his hand came out, holding her arm. "Will you stay a moment?"

Tanis looked up at the sky and her face was immediately spattered. Nevertheless, she nodded. Anything to make a sale, she thought. "Do you—do you want an explanation of them?" she asked.

"Thanks, but no. They're neither abstract nor obscure. Their meaning is clear. All the same, the artist's personality comes through." He turned to her, watching as she pushed her wet hair from her eyes. "What is your sister's name?"

"Cassandra." He seemed to be waiting. "Foster," she added. "Mine's Tanis Foster."

He nodded, appearing satisfied. His attention returned to the display and Tanis hoped that the rivulets of rain that ran down the clinging film did not hide the depth of Cassandra's artistic imagination, or conceal the maturity of her interpretation.

"Is your sister older than you?"

"No, she's younger by five years."

His question had revealed a perception that surprised her. She supposed that a few moments of standing beside someone in the pouring rain was hardly sufficient to enable her to make an analysis of anyone's character.

Or was it, she wondered, stealing a glance and liking his profile, the shoulders that spoke of strength enough to take the weight of responsibility, the capability inherent in the long-fingered hands that raked through his wayward hair. And she wondered, too, how it would be if those fingers had run through *her* hair, lingering, making physical contact....

Shocked by her own wayward thoughts, she turned away. He might by now have decided against buying but did not know how to extricate himself from the situation he had brought about by asking her to remain.

"Do I make out the check to you or to your sister?"

Tanis swung back, her face transformed. She had made a sale! "Oh, you're going to buy! To my sister, please." She consulted the price list excitedly. "Tell me which one."

"I'll tell you in my car."

Her hesitation was purely instinctive, born of fear, of terrors told through the media. "It's drier in the car."

His voice was dry, too. He added quietly, "You need have no fear of me."

At once she believed him. She nodded, turned and signaled to Edna, who watched with a frown. *How can I reassure her,* Tanis wondered, but knew it was impossible. Even words would not soothe her friend's suspicion, and rightly so, she thought. On the face of it, it seemed madness to get into a strange man's car; but mad or not, she did. As he closed the door and walked around to the driver's side, Tanis wished she had noted the car's registration number.

The amusement was there again, tinged with mockery. He reeled off the car's number as if he had guessed her thoughts. "My license, my bank card, my credit cards." He showed the items he had named. "Anything else you'd like to know?"

"Thank you, but no. It's stupid of me—"

"Not stupid at all, Miss Foster." He produced a check book, then a pen. He started to fill in the date. "An attractive girl like you can't be too careful." The smile he flashed at her made her heart leap like a horse over a hurdle. It banished the cool detachment from his features, replacing it with a warmth and animation that had a devastating effect on Tanis's feminine responses.

Tentatively she smiled back, just a little afraid—not of the stranger's character but of the hidden magnetism on which that brilliant smile had lifted a curtain. *Why am I worrying,* she asked herself. *After he's bought the picture he wants, I'll never see him again.*

"Which painting did you want, Mr.—"

"Barratt, Gregg Barratt."

"—Mr. Barratt, because I'll have to check on the price and then unfasten the painting." Her hand found the door catch. "It will need drying with a cloth, I'm afraid."

His hand was on her arm again and this time she was

acutely conscious of the man's touch. "Not it, Miss Foster. Them."

"Them?"

"Them. All of them."

Tanis pulled at the neck of her T-shirt as if she were choking. "Are you—are you joking, Mr. Barratt? I mean, no one has ever...no one could *afford* to buy—" A suspicion invaded her mind. "The paintings aren't cheap, Mr. Barratt, and there are fifteen of them. They're not rubbish. They're good."

"I know they are," was the reasoned answer, "otherwise I wouldn't be buying them."

Her eyes widened with the thought that had occurred. "Are you a gallery owner?"

He shook his head. "My house is large. Its walls are bare and badly need brightening with color, life, encapsulated movement."

"But—your wife, how do you know she'll approve of all those pictures?"

"I have no wife to either approve or disapprove. Which means I can please myself." His hand motioned to the pictures. "Have I given an acceptable reason for wanting them?" He smiled down at the checkbook, pen poised. "You're hardly a top-class saleswoman, are you, Miss Foster?"

Tanis blushed angrily. "I always do my best for my sister. Please make it out to Cassandra Foster. We'll need the price list to add up the amount."

As she searched for the door catch he was out of the car himself. Untying the string that attached the price list to the railings, he carried it back to the car and took the paper tissue that Tanis held out. He needed two to absorb the moisture.

Not one eyebrow lifted in question, even when the total cost came to a very high figure. Nor did he question the fact that an unknown artist should ask such prices for her work.

On the contrary, he commented, "Your sister is modest about the value of her paintings."

"It's the circumstances, isn't it? I mean—" she found his cool eyes upon her "—the rain, the road, the whole situation. You can't ask a good market price for a commodity displayed like that." She stared at the pictures.

"So I'm getting a bargain," he remarked conversationally.

"Well, I might be prejudiced, being her sister, but I think you are."

He was busy writing. "I've added a bit extra to bring the amount to a round figure."

A quick look revealed the sum he had written on the check. Frowning, she commented, "Is it really as much as that, Mr. Barratt? Are you sure you haven't made a mistake?"

"You don't trust my arithmetic?" He leaned across and felt in the glove compartment. "I hope you'll trust this." He took a pocket calculator from its case. "Watch as I punch out each amount. Come closer, Miss Foster. I don't eat strange young women. My job in life is to heal, not harm."

Tanis frowned. "You mean—you're a doctor?"

"A surgeon." He gave the information offhandedly. "Now watch." Line by line he punched out the prices, showing her the total. "Plus the bit I've added. It tallies, doesn't it—which proves that my brain is still funcitoning in spite of these things." He indicated the pocket calculator and put it away. He signed the check, turned it over and wrote his name and address on the back.

"Is that where you live?" Tanis asked. "Isn't that a village near Ashdown Forest?"

He nodded. "On the borders. I travel to London most days."

There was an unconscious wistfulness in her voice as

she commented, "It must be lovely to go home to that place every day."

He was putting his pen away. "Where do you and your sister live, Miss Foster?"

A sigh escaped her. She pointed back along the road. "South London." She named the town. "It's not a bad area, but where we live. . . . She shook her head.

"Do you have a telephone?"

"Yes. Why?"

He did not answer. Instead he handed her the check.

"I don't know how to thank you, Mr.—" she remembered his profession. "*Dr.* Barratt."

It was time to leave the shelter of his car. The rain had eased a little, but there was still the question of conveyance of the paintings to his home.

"There's a man I know at the nearby hospital. He owns a van. When I leave you I'll stop in there. He'll be along to collect the paintings just as soon as he can. Don't worry," he added with a smile as he opened his door, "he'll bring a soft cloth to dry them."

He went around to the passenger door and opened it. Tanis stood beside him under the gray skies that for the moment had stopped hurling down the rain. The time for parting had come and she was curiously reluctant to let him go. "I don't know how to thank you," she said again.

"Shouldn't I be thanking you and your sister? Today I found what for a long time I'd been looking for—something to brighten my life."

"Don't you mean your house?"

"Maybe both." He smiled and started to return to his car, then stopped. "Fred Harley will be along as soon as he can manage it." A hand came out. "Goodbye, Miss Foster. I've enjoyed meeting you. I would have been happy to have met the artist, too." His hand clasped hers firmly but briefly.

Tanis stared at the check, then lifted large serious

brown eyes to his. "She would love to have met you, Dr. Barratt. She always asks for a description of the people who buy her work. But, you see—" her eyes grew troubled "—she's an invalid."

Walking back to her friend, she left the man gazing after her.

THE MAN CALLED FRED HARLEY came within half an hour. He brought a cloth with him. Extra absorbent, he explained, dabbing gently at each picture as it was detached from the railings.

"They're real lovely, miss," Mr. Harley said. "Did you paint them?"

"My sister," she told him. "She'll be over the moon when I tell her they're all sold. Every single one." Her eyes shone. "I still can't believe it."

Fred Harley laughed. "He knows what's good, does Dr. Barratt." He added, "I've known him a long time. I'm a kind of odd-job man at the hospital. Dr. Barratt's been coming there to work for a good few years now, although he does seem to spend more time in London than he used to. But I think if he had his choice he'd rather work here full-time. He loves the country, you know."

"And oil paintings, from the look of it," Tanis put in, laughing.

Mr. Harley laughed with her. He was a thin, gray-haired man of medium height. His face was lined, as though he had known his share of grief and happiness.

"You're right—oil paintings, too." With great care he stacked the pictures in boxes in the van. "Well, it's been nice meeting you." He looked around him. "You must have wanted to sell those pictures real bad, coming out on a day like this. That your sister over there, miss?"

"That's my friend. My sister—she couldn't come. She's not well, you see."

Fred Harley frowned in sympathy but asked no questions. A few minutes later Tanis was watching the back of the van disappearing into the distance. She turned to find that Edna's father had come for her in his car. He was round faced and cheerful, like his daughter. They exchanged a few words about the weather, Edna called, "See you again sometime, maybe," and joined her father in the car. With a wave they drove away.

CASSANDRA GAVE A WHOOP OF JOY when Tanis told her the news. She flung her arms around Tanis's neck, then cried before she laughed with happiness.

"How much did it come to?" Cassandra asked when she had recovered. Tanis showed her the check and she went pale. "He must have got his sums wrong."

Tanis shook her head. "He added it up twice, once with his head and once with a pocket calculator. I watched him. He did add just a bit more, to bring it to round figures."

Cassandra gazed up at her wide-eyed. "I didn't know such philanthropy existed in this world anymore."

Tanis looked with tenderness at her sister as she sat in the wheelchair. People often said how alike they looked, but they saw only the surface features. Cassandra's hair was almost black, like her own. They shared brown eyes, too, but Cassandra's held an unquenchable optimism that even a serious car accident had not quelled.

Cassandra's face, again like Tanis's, narrowed from high cheekbones to a softly rounded chin, but in its upward curve her mouth revealed an undaunted optimism that her sister's did not. Tanis's nature, although warm and passionate, was more serious and restrained.

"You know what this money means, don't you?" Tanis reminded her sister. "That it won't be long now before we've got enough to pay for a really top specialist to perform the final operation that will let you walk almost normally again."

Cassandra grew thoughtful, fingering the check as if to assure herself that it was real. "Do you know, Tanis," she remarked, "I've discovered I've become a fatalist as well as an optimist. If that operation—when I have it—doesn't succeed, then—" she took a breath and let it out slowly "—I'll take it on the chin."

"You've got a funny idea of your anatomy," Tanis threw in, laughing.

Cassandra laughed with her. "But if it succeeds—" her eyes began to water and she dashed the moisture away "—well, I'll believe it when I see it. Feel it, I mean!"

Frank Anderson came that evening. Besides being Cassandra's boyfriend, he was Tanis's partner in the interior-decorating business they shared. He was tall and his narrow-shouldered build belied his inherent stamina. He was self-assured and pushing and was the half of the partnership that acquired most of the work that came their way. His hair was light brown, bleaching to fair after sessions of exterior painting in the sun.

Since Cassandra had met him, about nine months before her accident, she had thought the sun shone out of his eyes. She had wanted only his company. Tanis's greatest fear was that one day he might walk out of her sister's life and never return.

If it ever happened, it would leave Cassandra devastated and herself partnerless, having either to abandon the business or carry on single-handed. And that, she knew, would mean the end, because who, she reasoned, would employ a young woman to do a job that in the past had traditionally been associated with men?

So when Frankie, after kissing Cassandra lightly on the lips, sauntered to Tanis's side and put his arm around her waist, she did not repel him as every instinct urged her to do. Instead she summoned a smile and

said, "Howdy, pardner," and pretended to slap paint up and down his face with an imaginary brush.

Wondering how to detach herself from Frankie's hold, she seized on his shift of attention to Cassandra, who said, "Guess what, Frankie? Tanis has sold all my pictures. All of them at one go." She made a sweeping motion. "Just like that."

"Hey, that's fantastic. Who was the great benefactor?"

Tanis went to Cassandra's side. Frankie would not touch her there.

"A man," Cassandra informed him. "A kind and wonderful man."

"What are you going to do with the money?"

"You know very well, Frank Anderson," Cassandra scolded. "Pay for that very important operation on my legs."

"The one that should make her able to walk almost normally again," Tanis added.

"What, *another* operation?"

"Don't say it like that!" Cassandra's response held anguish. "It sounds as if you're doubting whether the operation will succeed. Don't kill the only thing I've got."

"And what might that be?" Frankie's question was spoken stiffly. Was he afraid, Tanis wondered, that she might say "You"?

"Hope, that's what."

Yes, there was the relief in his face. Tanis turned away, sickened by Frankie's attitude. When Cassandra had first known him he was loving and possessive, talking of their future together. Since the accident and Cassandra's confinement to a wheelchair, he had changed toward her, but so subtly that she hadn't even noticed.

But Tanis knew. She knew by the way she had, on a number of occasions, fought off his attentions herself.

The worrying thing was that if she really told him what she thought of him for his offhand attitude toward her sister, and for his secret pursuit of herself, he would walk out and leave them both abandoned high and dry.

Cassandra put out her hand to Frankie. "You haven't congratulated me yet. Aren't I a clever girl?"

He put her hand in his and squeezed it, then she tugged him down, holding up her face for his kiss. It was an act of complete trust, with a little-girl touch that was quite unconscious.

Watching them, Tanis saw Frankie's kiss, which Cassandra had plainly expected to be a quick salute to her success, turn into something far more demanding. Knowing her sister as well as she did, she could read surprise in the widening of Cassandra's young brown eyes and the stiffening of her hand on the chair arm.

She's too young, Tanis thought, turning away. *Frankie's twenty-four. He's crammed more experience into the four-year gap between them than Cassandra will ever know.*

When Tanis turned back, she saw that her sister's face was flushed and a hand was pressed to her mouth. But her eyes held unmistakable pleasure.

"I'll make some coffee," Tanis said, going into the kitchen.

Frankie followed, saying, "Not much work around at the moment, is there?"

Tanis arranged the mugs for use. "Might be because a lot of people are into D.I.Y."

"Yeah. Not much good for our business, though, is it? Think we could get a leaflet printed? One that goes something like, 'Do-it-yourself is okay if you don't mind the mess hanging around for weeks, and if you're willing to use up your precious spare time slapping on wallpaper and paint. If not, why not let the experts do it? Experts like Anderson and Foster—'"

"Foster and Anderson," Tanis corrected with a smile.

She watched as the kettle came to the boil, her back to her business partner. When two arms caught her around the waist, she jumped violently, then stood passive, hoping it would make him loosen his hold.

"Anderson and Foster," Frankie repeated. "Fight you for it."

Yes, that's just what you'd like, Tanis thought, *a fight so that you could win and....* "Have it your way," she managed to sigh, glad that Cassandra could not see her boyfriend's inconstant behavior.

Breaking free, she made the coffee and said, "It would cost money."

"What would?"

"Forgotten already?"

As Tanis finished pouring the coffee, a face swam before her eyes and she hardly noticed Frankie taking the tray into the living room. It was the face of the man she would never see again. Yet the image persisted as if the imprinting of his features on her memory was in itself a magic charm to bring him back into her life.

"Having leaflets printed," Tanis said, entering the living room and speaking as if the conversation had never been interrupted.

"Oh, that," Frankie laughed. "I meant it only as a joke."

"Meant what?" Cassandra asked, sipping her coffee, then looking up adoringly at Frankie's profile as he sat beside her. He ruffled her hair, then explained about his idea for the promotion of their business.

His attitude to Cassandra, Tanis observed as she watched them, was more like that of a brother than a boyfriend. *Can't she see,* she wondered. *Is she really so inexperienced in the ways of men that she doesn't realize how much her accident has changed Frankie's attitude toward her?*

"I think it might be a good idea," Tanis insisted. "Any form of advertising is better than none."

"Who'd do the pushing through mailboxes? Count me out," Frankie told her irritably.

"Couldn't we give some schoolchildren a bit of extra pocket money to do it for us?"

Frankie lifted careless shoulders. "Tell you what, I'll go and tackle that outside painting job tomorrow, weather permitting. You draft out the leaflet and take it to the local printer and talk about it with him. Get an estimate of his charges, quantity, size and so on. Okay?" He pulled himself out of the chair. "I'll be off."

Cassandra caught his hand. "A kiss before you go."

There was the faintest hesitation, which only Tanis saw. Bending down and obliging, Frankie commented, "Regular little nymphomaniac you are, Cassandra Foster."

Cassandra giggled. Then with an exaggerated movement she wiped the cheek that Frankie's lips had touched. "You're not a Casanova, that's for sure," she informed him ruefully.

"You're hardly in a state to entertain me if I were," he threw back callously.

Tanis, seeing her sister flinch, felt the pain as her own.

CHAPTER TWO

TOWARD THE END OF THE WEEK the leaflets were drafted and their layout approved by the printer. He had promised to have them ready by early the following week.

The weather had remained good enough for Frankie to make some progress with the outside painting job. Leaving Cassandra immersed in working out ideas for a new picture, Tanis had joined him, painting the downstairs and allowing him, for once, to climb the ladders.

It was the weekend again, and in the spare moments between attending to Cassandra, bed making and preparing the lunch, Tanis allowed her thoughts to wander again to the man who by buying Cassandra's paintings had brought them so much hope. A benefactor, Frankie had called him. Was that what he was, Tanis wondered. Had he purchased the paintings out of the kindness of his heart, or had he really needed them to brighten the walls of his home?

Did it matter, she asked herself with a sigh, staring out onto the shabby street that was lined with even shabbier houses, most of which had been, like theirs, turned into separate apartments. The whole house had been their mother's. When she had died it had become theirs, meaning that, unlike thousands of other people, they would always have a roof over their heads. The only way they could maintain the place adequately, they had decided, was to rent out the upper floor.

This they had done, and there was now a middle-aged widow in residence. Tanis and her sister occupied the

ground floor, making the old dining room into a bedroom that they shared.

Cars lined the curbs on both sides of the street. There was rarely a space outside the house, but that morning it happened that there was. As Tanis gazed out, a car slid into view. It was large and familiar. With skill the driver maneuvered the vehicle into the empty parking place.

It was the driver who had Tanis's mind reeling and her heart pounding like a hammer on a nail. He couldn't, she thought, he just couldn't come in with the place in such a mess! There were newspapers everywhere, magazines and Cassandra's abandoned sketches that had floated to the floor.

"Cassie," Tanis said hoarsely, shortening her sister's name, which in itself was sufficient to reveal to Cassandra her distress, "he's coming. That man—he's almost at the door. And look at the place, just look!"

Mildly surprised at her sister's agitation, Cassandra asked, "What man?" Understanding dawned. "Not the one who—"

"That one." There was a cracked ring at the door. The bell needed replacing. "Oh, heavens—" she looked down at herself "—I'm a mess. My clothes, my hair—"

"Open it," Cassandra cried. "The door—let him in. I want to say thank—"

"The door was on the catch," the visitor said, "so I walked in." A quizzical eyebrow lifted at Tanis's obvious confusion.

When it registered that he was here, the man whose face had superimposed itself on everything she had looked at, every page of every book, every hero of every television film, a smile broke out that was like sunshine flooding the earth after a downpour.

"Dr. Barratt," she said, "you're welcome, very welcome."

He gave a small mocking bow.

"Dr. Barratt," Cassandra's voice came urgently from

around the door that hid him, "I'm so glad you've come. I want—" She stared. "Oh, my!" She clapped a hand to her mouth, but her eyes roved over him from head to tail. "No wonder Tanis has been mooning over you the whole week."

"Cassandra, I haven't!" Her indignation came from a throat tight with embarrassment. *Sometime,* she thought, *Cassie will play the naive little sister once too often.* She lifted a flushed face to the visitor. "Dr. Barratt, I was intending to write to you...." She frowned. "But I haven't yet, so how did you know our address?"

"I asked if you had a telephone. From there it was easy." He moved around the door and stood, hands in pockets, frowning. "Wheelchair, Miss Foster? You didn't tell me."

"I said Cassandra was an invalid, so why are you looking at me as though I've committed a crime?" A moment's probing and her brain had the answer. She smiled. "It's the doctor in you, isn't it? So I forgive you."

"I'm greatly relieved," he commented dryly. "I might have had a sleepless night without your forgiveness."

The sarcasm grated, and she frowned. "That's the man speaking, and—I'm not sure I like him."

He laughed, but his eyes did not crinkle. "You don't know the man in me, Miss Foster."

He was darned right, she didn't! Nor was she sure she wanted to. Where was the kindly philanthropist who had sat beside her in that large car he owned, writing a check the amount of which had left her gasping and full of joy at the prospect of her sister's eventual cure coming a giant step nearer?

"Dr. Barratt, you're an angel." Cassandra's hand reached out to grasp him. "You don't mind if I...?" She was pressing the back of his hand to her cheek. "Oh, Dr. Barratt, if you knew how I hate having to sit

in this chair day after day watching Tanis do everything, work all hours to feed us, clothe us, and me not able to do anything to help.''

The kindliness was back in his face for Cassandra. ''You paint, Miss Foster. The pictures sell, which means you earn money.''

''It's Cassandra, not Miss Foster.'' She made a face. ''And that money's for me, not for general use. For—for the operation that will get me back on my feet. I'm on a list, a long, long list at the local hospital. One of hundreds of patients who are waiting.''

Gregg Barratt did not seem to understand and turned to Tanis, eyebrows raised.

Hesitant in view of the status of their visitor, Tanis explained, ''We thought that if we could save up enough from the sale of Cassandra's pictures, we'd be able to go to a specialist and pay him to treat her.''

''It would cost hundreds.'' There was deep concern in the words.

''We've been saving for ages, Dr. Barratt,'' Cassandra put in. ''And thanks to your buying all those paintings of mine, we're a lot nearer our target. Dr. Barratt—'' she tugged him lower ''—do you mind if I give you a thank-you kiss? Just a little one, here on your cheek.'' The kiss was implanted and tears sprang in her eyes, remaining unshed.

For a long moment Gregg Barratt looked down at the girl, compassion deepening the amber of his eyes. She gazed up at him, unconsciously childlike in her instant trust in him. He was that kind of man, Tanis found herself thinking. Hadn't she instinctively trusted him last Sunday when he had invited her into his car?

''I want to thank you, too, Dr. Barratt.'' Tanis's voice was small, her smile tight. ''You don't know how we've appreciated your gesture in—''

He was moving toward her, appearing not to have heard the halting words. There was a look in his eyes

that had Tanis backing away. He hadn't looked at
Cassandra like that, she thought, dismayed. "No, no.
You misunderstood me. I meant thank you verbally,
Dr. Barratt."

He seemed to have become deaf, but was smiling a
wicked smile. Now she was out of the door and in the
hall. He caught her there, his hands grasping her upper
arms. "I'm an eager receiver of thanks in the form of
kisses, Miss Foster. And not just on the cheek. Here will
do."

There was no chance to utter a word of protest. His
mouth was on hers, not with gentleness but with a demand that had her clinging to the broad solidity of his
shoulders, had her heartbeats racing and her lungs crying out for air. She came up gasping. "How could you
do that?" she asked, her fingers shaking as they pressed
her bruised lips.

His hands dropped away, finding his jacket pockets.
He was smiling as he said, "It's the man in me,
Miss Foster. You know that man a little better now
than you did earlier. Do you 'like' him any better,
too?"

A hand still covered her mouth, and she shook her
head. "That wasn't a man kissing me. It was an—an
animal." Even she realized that was going a bit far.

"Animal?" he exclaimed. "Good grief, if I really let
the animal in me loose on you, you'd wonder what had
hit you."

"Dr. Barratt?" Cassandra calling from the living
room broke into the tense atmosphere.

Gregg Barratt swung away and joined her. Tanis held
back, seeking for composure, taming her indignation at
the stranger's assault on her mouth and her dignity.
Slowly she followed him and heard Cassandra say,
"You're a surgeon, aren't you? Well—" excitement
lighted the eager brown eyes "—would *you* be able to
treat me?"

"Cassie!" Tanis ran across to her. "What are you saying?"

Gregg lowered himself to his haunches beside Cassandra's chair. He looked at her thin legs and her feet on the chair's footrest, then smiled up into her face. "There's no need for your sister to be so shocked." His hand covered Cassandra's. "I'm flattered that you should place so much trust in me on such a short acquaintance. Maybe your sister doesn't share that trust."

"Oh, but I do, I do!"

His head turned and his smile mocked Tanis's outburst, then his attention returned to Cassandra.

"Dr. Barratt—" bright earnest eyes pleaded "—if... if you could, and if you could make me better, really better, my boyfriend would love me again and—"

"You mean he's stopped loving you? Because of this?" He indicated her legs.

"He...he...." She cast an anguished look at her sister. "Tanis and he—"

"Tanis?" Hearing her name spoken with anger by the man whose powerful attraction she had been unable to forget since her first meeting with him made Tanis go cold. "You mean she's taken your boyfriend from you?"

"No, no!" Now the anguish was in Tanis's eyes. "You misunderstand. He's my partner, my business partner. That's what Cassie means, isn't it, Cassie?"

There was a silent appeal for understanding in the look she directed at her sister. Had Cassandra noticed more than she had thought? Had she seen Frankie's sly kisses, his hand perpetually seeking her waist, and worst, her failure to repulse him for fear that he might desert them both?

Cassandra swallowed and stared down at her clenched hands. "Yes, that's what I meant. You—you did misunderstand, Dr. Barratt. Frankie's my boy-

friend, not Tanis's. He—he still loves me, I . . . I think.
She's right; they run a business together.''

"Business?" He straightened. "What kind of
business?" There was no kindliness in the tone or the
hard look.

"Interior decoration," Tanis answered.

"You, an interior decorator?"

Tanis had heard it all before. "Meaning that because
I'm a woman—" she repeated words she had used so
often to defend her job "—I'm not capable of tackling
the hard work involved, or climbing ladders to the dizzy
heights of the guttering outside?"

"Every man Tanis tells," Cassandra explained,
"reacts in the same way as you."

"I'm duly crushed," Gregg Barratt retaliated mockingly. "I accept the rebuke implied in your answer.
Satisfied?" Tanis smiled and nodded. "So Cassandra's boyfriend," he went on, "is your business partner
and he hasn't stopped loving her." He indicated
Cassandra.

How was it possible to answer such a question truth-
fully when she knew what Cassandra also appeared to
know—that Frankie's attitude had changed after the
accident? "He—I . . . ." In desperation Tanis changed
the subject, noting as she did so the faint cruelty in
Gregg Barratt's smile. "Would you be able to do as
Cassandra asked and—" She stopped, realizing that
probably medical ethics would prevent such a request
from being successful.

"Would I what?" The question sounded impatient,
which confused her even more.

"I know it would be impossible." Her smile was tight
as she finished, "A dream come true. And dreams just
don't come true, do they, Dr. Barratt? Not in real life."

He left Cassandra's side and walked across to stand in
front of Tanis. "We're onto dreams now, are we? I
thought we were discussing surgery for your sister.

Unfortunately for both of you, my speciality is obstetrics.''

"Oh." Tanis's smile was weak. "Women's illnesses, childbirth and—and things?"

He nodded and returned to Cassandra. "You need the services of an orthopedic surgeon." His fist tossed her chin. "Don't look so downhearted. Will you keep on hoping?" His smile was persuasive, and Cassandra responded in full to the charm.

"And saving," she took him up eagerly. "Which means I must paint as fast as I can."

"Not so fast that you ruin the quality of your work. For someone so young, you have a considerable insight into life."

"Maybe it was my accident?" She frowned as if her thoughts hurt. "The pain, the discomfort and then the...." She indicated the wheelchair, then herself.

"The restriction on your movements," Gregg supplied, "the imprisonment of your young and active body?"

Cassandra nodded eagerly. "You're very understanding, aren't you?" Again her hand came out and grasped his. She gazed up at him with something near to adoration. "I'm sure it was magic that made you appear at Tanis's stand and see my paintings. Then you came today and...and...." Color was reddening her cheeks. "I think—do you know what I think?"

Solemnly Gregg shook his head.

"I think," Cassandra went on, "that you're something I can hold on to. Dr. Barratt—" her eyes moistened again "—you give me courage and hope. Hope that one day I'll be able to get out of this chair and be free again—free! That—" she swallowed and rubbed her eyes "—will be a wonderful day. A dream come true, in fact."

Tanis held her breath. Was he going to remind Cassandra of how her sister had said only a few minutes

earlier that dreams did not come true? To Tanis's relief, it seemed not.

"Cassandra—" he crouched again "—your faith in me overpowers me. I only wish I could be the one to give you back that freedom."

"It doesn't matter that you can't, Dr. Barratt. As long as you don't just—disappear from my life as quickly as you came into it." It was as though the words were too terrible to be spoken.

"Dr. Barratt," Tanis said hurriedly, her eyes deeply brown with the desire to offer him an escape route if he wanted one, "she—I . . . ." Gregg stood, hands in pockets, refusing to help her with the appropriate words as he had helped Cassandra. "Please don't feel under any obligation to my sister or myself," she went on. "Cassandra only meant—"

"I know exactly what your sister meant." His glance went to Cassandra, then back to Tanis. "Your parents—do they live elsewhere?"

Tanis shook her head. "My mother was a widow. She died shortly before Cassandra's accident." A frown of sympathy pleated Gregg Barratt's forehead. "This house was hers and she left it to us. We've rented out the upper floor to a widow. She looks after Cassandra when I'm out."

He nodded, his eyes passing over the faded furniture and carpets.

"Why did you come, Dr. Barratt?" Cassandra asked as he went to the door.

"To see the artist, the girl who created the paintings I've bought."

"Were you disappointed?" Cassandra's smile was mischievous.

"On the contrary, delighted." With a warm smile at Cassandra and a brief nod to Tanis, he was in the hall and out of the house before Tanis could move or speak a final word of thanks.

Two evenings later Frankie phoned. He was too tired, he told Tanis, after a hard day's work to join her in delivering leaflets.

"Even though it might bring us more work?" she returned. "The leaflets were your idea."

"I didn't mean it seriously. You went ahead and got them printed."

"Meaning I deliver them, too? All right, I will, but you're miserable, Frankie Anderson. For two pins I'd find myself another partner."

"Remind me to give you two pins."

Fear had her saying, "Don't be silly; you know I didn't mean it."

"That changed your tune," Frankie sneered. "Mind what you say in future. You'd hate Cassandra to be hurt again, wouldn't you? And don't say you don't know what I mean."

"I know what you mean, you rotten, horrible—" Raucous laughter cut her off.

"Hey, Tanis," Cassandra's wavering voice came from the living room, "that's my boyfriend you're talking to."

Tanis took a breath and said in a conciliatory tone, "Frankie, I . . . ." The phone went dead.

The next-door neighbor's two children happily accompanied Tanis on her rounds. The brother and sister took a pile of leaflets each, going along one side of the road while Tanis worked along the other. On the way back Tanis bought the children ice-cream cones.

"That should bring in some work," Tanis announced as she closed the front door. Cassandra was where she had left her—painting in the living room. But she was not alone. Gregg Barratt lounged in an armchair.

His thick brown hair had been raked back. Broad shoulders stretched a black, high-necked sweater. A bronze-colored shirt collar showed above it, complementing the fascinating shade of his eyes. The creased,

tight-fitting brown slacks outlined the muscularity of his thighs as his legs thrust forward over the hearth rug.

His indolent attitude and cynical smile as he looked interestedly at the curves beneath Tanis's yellow T-shirt was so much at variance with his customary autocratic bearing that she gazed at him bemused.

As she entered the room, Gregg glanced behind her. "No business partner in tow? You don't mean you delivered a pile of leaflets alone?"

Tanis explained stiffly that the next-door children had helped her.

"Frankie wouldn't come," Cassandra added. "Said he was too tired after a day's work."

"He said he only suggested the leaflets as a joke," Tanis took her up, "but I went ahead and got them printed."

"So he bounced the ball back into your court." Tanis nodded. Gregg stretched and rested his head on his linked hands. Tanis felt the tug of his looks, the desire to touch his sensually full mouth. "You should get yourself another partner."

"I can't. He's so good at his job." There was, she realized, a kind of anguish in her voice. Gregg's uplifted brow told her he had heard it and misinterpreted it as anxiety arising from the fear of losing Frankie for emotional and not business reasons.

"Frankie's a genius," Cassandra enlarged. Gregg smiled at what he construed to be hero worship of her boyfriend. "He's as much an artist as I am. And don't smile like that, Dr. Barratt. I mean it, not as his girl but as a fellow artist. Ask Tanis. She knows what I mean."

Tanis nodded. "Really, Frankie's wasted on commonplace things like outside work. He's an expert on interior design. He knows all about the importance of color, and about wall fabrics and lighting effect. He came up the hard way. He started straight out of school,

but someone told him he had that extra something, so he left his job and took it from there.''

Gregg's hands found his pockets. His smile was twisted as he raked Tanis with his analytical gaze. "You seem to find him as irresistible as your sister does.''

"You've got it wrong, Dr. Barratt. He's not my type.''

"Oh?'' The questioner slid lower in his seat, the movement tautening his slacks across his thighs and strong-boned hips. "What kind of man is your type?''

You. The word sprang unexpectedly. Was this man her type? There was no denying the increase in her pulse rate, the speeding of her body's metabolism when she set eyes on him, or merely thought about him. Yet his character was as much an enigma now as the day she had met him.

"She's had boyfriends,'' her sister supplied. "I've lost count. They've come and they've gone, haven't they Tanis?''

"Have they?'' Tanis answered without interest.

"But as far as I can remember,'' Cassandra persisted, "there's been no particular hair coloring or characteristic common to them all.''

"All shapes and sizes, you'd say,'' Gregg commented, amusement lurking in his narrowed eyes. "What's the current one like?''

"There isn't one,'' Tanis answered shortly. She turned challenging, bold eyes to her questioner. The message was silent but clear: *don't bring Frankie Anderson into this. He's not mine; he's Cassandra's.*

Again the dark brows moved upward, eyes skeptical.

Tanis swung away, turned back. "Would you like a drink, Dr. Barratt?''

"Cassandra offered me one and I helped myself, thanks.'' He lifted himself high in the chair.

As Tanis poured herself a glass of fruit juice in the kitchen, she heard Gregg ask, "What happened when you fell off your bicycle?''

Cassandra answered, "The motorbike that I'd veered left to avoid went out of the driver's control. He rode over me, around me and still couldn't regain control. Would you believe it, he rode over me again. All the time I was screaming, of course."

"He drove over her legs," Tanis said, joining them and sitting in the other armchair. "The man finally came off and he was injured, too, but not at all as badly as Cassandra."

Gregg Barratt, trained to reveal nothing of his emotions, appeared unmoved, but it was plain he was thinking about the situation. "I assume you had numerous operations?"

"Weeks in hospital," Tanis told him. "Home again, then in again. Each time a little more was done. But she's still in that chair."

"I want to get out of it, Dr. Barratt." Cassandra's voice rose. "I want to be able to walk, go dancing with Frankie. You know what I mean?"

"I know how it is, Cassandra." Gregg did not hide his sympathy now.

"That's why we're saving," Tanis offered. "To find a really good specialist."

"And be able to pay any fee he asks, as long as he can free me from this chair."

There was a long silence. Gregg's head was against the chair back. His eyes were open, but he was so deep in thought it was as if he were in another world. Tanis put her glass down quietly, like someone afraid of arousing a sleeper. *When is he going to speak,* she wondered.

At last he roused himself, stood up and walked around. "I have a suggestion to make." Tanis watched the tall, lean figure striding restlessly, fisted hands filling his trouser pockets, tugging at the brown fabric across his hips.

He swung to face them, his face serious. "My house is

large. I haven't lived there long. There are a number of rooms, furnished but unoccupied. I have a housekeeper and her husband in residence. They're both capable, efficient—and bored.''

He resumed his walking. Tanis followed his every movement, her breathing tight. He turned again, this time directing his words at her.

"My suggestion is this. Those rooms need filling. My two employees need work to keep them busy. You and your sister could provide that work—by coming to live in my house.''

Tanis, her limbs stiff with tension, took a furtive glance at her sister. Cassandra's eyes were wider than ever; her delicately molded mouth was parted, her hands gripping the chair arms.

Her own feelings, Tanis reflected, were simple to analyze. She was astonished, unbelieving—and filled with a pure delight. Yet she could not speak a word. All the time Gregg Barratt watched her, no longer the indolent, slightly lecherous male. He had climbed into his aloof man-of-medicine skin. There was no way of tearing off that clinical mask and penetrating to the masculine, warmly human man inside.

"Turn the suggestion down if you like," he said without expression, having waited a few moments for some response. "My feelings are neutral." Again he waited and Tanis wondered at his patience. "It would," he continued, still addressing her, "get Cassandra into a better environment. She would have constant attention. There would be a view of the gardens fine enough to inspire her even in her least productive moods. Well—" he glanced from one to the other "—what do you say?''

Cassandra stared at Tanis as if every part of her body was willing her to speak. "Say something, Tanis," she said at last. "Tell Dr. Barratt yes or no. But, Tanis—" her hand came out and Tanis touched it "—tell him yes, please, for my sake.''

"There's my work, Cassie. The decorating business. What about that? If I let that go, where would our income come from?"

"My house is just over twenty miles from here, Miss Foster. I assume that you have something like a van?"

"It's Frankie's, not mine."

He approached slowly, his expression unreadable as his glance flicked over her face. The cool deep brown of her eyes seemed to intrigue him, her perfectly shaped mouth, her pert nose and rounded chin putting words onto the blank screen of his face. But they faded out before she could grasp their meaning.

"Couldn't your partner come for you?" he asked at last. "If not, you could travel by train. Don't invent difficulties. Now, will you give me an answer?"

"It's kind of you, Dr. Barratt—" she met his gaze unflinchingly "—but could you give us time to talk about it?"

"No, no," Cassandra urged. "There's nothing to discuss. I want to accept. I want to get away from this place. You're not stuck here, Tanis, as I am, all day, every day, seeing that same old view, watching the parked cars—why, they're not even *moving*. Sometimes I try to paint but nothing comes. There's just no inspiration, no incentive, nothing to get my imagination working. Do you understand?" she finished earnestly.

"I understand, Cassie." Tanis rested her hand on her sister's shoulder. "I'd like to move from here, too, but—"

"Well, then?" Cassandra's large brown eyes, so like her own it was almost uncanny, were full of appeal.

"What are you waiting for, Miss Foster?"

The clipped question had her swinging to face Gregg Barratt. "There's the matter of my work, that's all."

His shoulders lifted and fell. "If you're so devoted to the interests of your business partner that you refuse to find a solution, or even a compromise, then at least let

your sister accept on her own behalf. She can come and you stay here.''

"I wouldn't go anywhere without Tanis.''

"Well—'' Gregg gave a short impatient sigh ''—I guess that's that.''

"No, it's not. Don't go, Dr. Barratt. Tanis, Frankie can't have it all his way. He's often told us to find somewhere better to live. Once he even asked me—'' her face turned a fiery red and she stared at her clasped hands ''—to go and live in his place. You know, share it.''

"You mean to live with him?'' Tanis's words came out in a dismayed whisper.

Cassandra nodded.

"Before your accident?'' Gregg asked sharply.

"Of course.'' Cassandra's color had receded. "Since then he. . . .'' Her eyes slid to her sister, then quickly away.

Gregg's glance followed closely and narrowly. Tanis knew what he was thinking. "Since then,'' she finished her sister's sentence, "life's changed for her so much it's almost as if she were another girl. She's lost her mobility, her independence—''

"Don't you think you're being cruel to your sister,'' Gregg reprimanded her, "holding up a cracked mirror for her to look in?''

Tanis gave him a fighting glance, then told her sister, "I didn't mean it that way. You know me better than that, don't you?''

Cassandra nodded, but the sad expression remained. Then she came to life and her eyes danced. "Persuade her, Dr. Barratt. Make her say 'Yes, we'll come.'''

"Make her?'' He took on Cassandra's mood and his eyes gleamed. "*Make* her? Yes, the idea appeals.'' He stood up. As he advanced, Tanis retreated. His hands slipped from his pockets and caught Tanis's arms. "This way, I think—man to woman, heart to heart.''

"Oh, no!" Tanis twisted away and turned and ran, followed by her sister's delighted laughter. Footsteps thudded behind her. She reached the kitchen and swung the door, but his weight was too heavy for her to hold him back.

His fingers were around her arms again and his eyes roamed her body as he held her away from him. "You look like a gamin, an urchin."

"These are my working clothes. I didn't bother to change before I went out. If I'd known we were going to have a visitor, a *distinguished* visitor, I—" mischief glowed in her brown eyes "—I still wouldn't have changed!"

Again she tried to escape, but he halted her struggles easily. His hold tightened and he pulled her unhurriedly against him. "It's your mind I intend to change, not your clothes. I've had permission from your sister to make you say yes." Speculation intensified the gleam in his eyes. "Will you say yes?"

He had shifted subtly from the subject and was laughing at her annoyance. "I'm sure you've got an address book full of women who'll say yes. My name's not joining theirs."

She stirred against the strength of him and was dismayed by her own bodily responses. Hard fingers moved and pushed up her chin. Piercing eyes probed her, then her mouth was taken by his. His lips parted hers and he savored the freshness within. Her hands were flat to his chest but grew weaker in their resistance. To her dismay, they began of their own volition to make their way to his shoulders, then to pass each other around his neck.

He swung her slightly to one side, moving one of his arms from around her. The free hand settled momentarily, fingers lightly outspread, against her throat. Obediently her head tipped back even farther as she eagerly accepted the deepening demand of his kiss.

When the roaming hand moved again, tracing her outline from shoulder to waist, her fingers pushed into the dark thickness of his hair. The cupping of his hand over her breast brought a gasp at his audacity and an increase in the agitated movement of her fingers in his hair. A warmth spread through her limbs, and as he moved into even closer contact she yielded with even greater eagerness to his caressing hands and lips.

He lifted her, allowing her mouth to ease away from his, but his hand stayed in undisputed possession. "Agree to my suggestion, urchin," he commanded. "Come and live with me."

Dazed by the aftereffects of his assault on her mouth and still aroused by his stroking touch, she could only look at him wide-eyed.

"Agree, bright eyes. Say, 'Yes, I agree.'"

"Whew." There was a low whistle from behind them. Frankie had used the key Tanis had given him to enter unobserved. "Freeze that frame."

Tanis broke away, breathing quickly, angry at the intrusion.

"It wouldn't pass the censor," Frankie commented. There was a sneer mixed with his smile. "What girl could say no after that hot scene?"

Tanis's hands hit her hips. Frustration and indignation made an explosive mix. "Get out of here, Frankie Anderson!" she ordered. "It's none of your business."

Gregg's arms folded across his chest. His smile was like that of a cat that had got at the cream and seen some more across the table. "Ah, but it could be," he said.

CHAPTER THREE

"NONE OF MY BUSINESS?" Frankie took up Tanis's remark. "When he's asking you to go and live with him? It darn well is. You're my business partner. Foster and Anderson. Remember?"

Tanis smiled grimly. "Thanks for putting me first for once. And Dr. Barratt was not inviting me to live with him."

"Yes, I was." This time the smile was like that of a cat licking spilled cream from its paws.

"There you are, then," said Frankie.

Now Tanis faced Gregg, head back, eyes stormy. "No, you weren't, not in that sense." To Frankie, "Dr. Barratt has just offered Cassandra and me a new home in his house, near Ashdown Forest in Sussex. It's a big house, he said, with lots of empty rooms—"

"Needing occupying," Gregg inserted.

"—and a housekeeper and her husband—"

"Needing occupying," Gregg repeated. His smile, this time directed at Tanis, taunted. By now Frankie, looking from one to the other, seemed a little bewildered.

"Dr. Barratt said," Tanis went on, irritated to find herself on the defensive, "that it would be a healthier environment for Cassandra. She'd be looked after when I'm not there, when I'm busy working...with you, of course. I'd—I'd need you more than ever, Frankie. As my partner, that is."

Now I'm appealing to him, she reproached herself, *but if he says, "Right, that's it; we go our separate*

ways," I'll have no work, couldn't pay the rent for our accommodation or our keep.

"That's fine, then," Frankie answered. Tanis's heart sank. So Frankie was opting out, after all? Then she realized he might have spoken in support of the idea, not against it. "You move out of this dump—"

"It's not a dump!" Cassandra called from the hall, having maneuvered herself there. "It was our mother's house. It was all she had to leave us."

Frankie joined her and Cassandra's arms reached up for him. Smoothly he went into them, kissing her upturned lips. "Do you want to go and live in a big house in the country?" he asked, pushing the chair back into the living room.

"Yes, oh, yes. And, Frankie, there's a beautiful view and I could paint and paint—"

"And what about me?" Frankie's smile was crooked and charming, but was there the faintest hint of a strain?

"You?" Cassandra frowned. "Well, you could come and see me. I mean, you'll still be Tanis's partner, won't you?"

"Will I?" He turned to Tanis, who stood behind him. Gregg Barratt had propped himself against the doorway.

Tanis stared at Frankie. Had she been right? Had he been backing out and not accepting the idea as she had hoped? "You mean," she said, "that if Cassie and I move out of this district—" she kept her voice steady, but even so her eyes gave away her worry "—you'll break up our partnership and form your own company?"

"I haven't said that, have I?" His hand caught hers, trapping her. It was a gesture that could convey either the irresistable attraction of the girl for the man, or the wish to reaffirm a good business relationship.

It seemed, by his cynical smile, that Gregg Barratt

had taken it the first way. Cassandra, wearing the dismayed look of a child watching a toy boat float out of reach downstream, seemed to agree with Gregg. Which, Tanis calculated, Frankie no doubt intended.

"Do you really think I'd break up Foster and Anderson?" he queried with apparent innocence, holding up their linked hands for Cassandra and the sardonically smiling visitor to see. "It's an ideal partnership. You do the dirty work, the everyday boring stuff, while I do the fancy work and chat up the beautiful wives of the big-city tycoons and charge them for the time I spend talking to them."

"You're a cunning, unprincipled rogue," Tanis scolded, shaking her hand free of his.

"That's right," Frankie replied jauntily. "I've got all the makings of your rich, successful businessman."

"You said it," Tanis returned bitterly.

"And it doesn't put you in a very good light," Cassandra reprimanded him.

"So you don't want me to be your boyfriend anymore? Okay—" he made for the door "—I'll get out of your lives. Both of you."

Gregg moved to make way for him, still smiling. Cassandra squealed in anguish.

"Come back here, Frankie," Tanis shrieked, running after him.

Frankie stopped, came back and laughed out loud. "I've got you both where I want you, haven't I?" he remarked, his beaming face full of self-congratulation. "You're both puppets on my string."

"You're a bigheaded, no-good cheat, Frankie Anderson," Tanis accused, mad at herself for revealing to him how much she relied on him—and thus, she feared, giving him a powerful weapon with which to taunt both herself and her sister.

As if to underline his power, and proving Tanis's fears to be real, his arms snaked around her waist. He

pulled her close and kissed her. In the circumstances she dared not repulse him nor even put on a token show of resistance, because if she did he might walk through that door and this time not return.

When Frankie moved from her and bent low into Cassandra's waiting arms to kiss her, too, Tanis stole a look at Gregg. The icy gaze he turned on her made her shiver inside. She gave glare for glare, thinking, *does he really believe I'm out to steal Frankie from Cassandra?*

His lack of faith in her integrity saddened her, since her faith in his could not be higher. There was far more to her feelings for this man, comparative stranger though he was, than mere liking or even attraction. Something inside her wanted to please him, to arouse him as he was able to arouse her, to make him admire her not as a gamin but as a desirable woman.

Tanis saw Frankie to the door. "So you don't mind if we move into the country?" she asked him, still a little uneasy about his response. "It's only about twenty miles away, Dr. Barratt said."

"That's okay with me," he said offhandedly. "We'll work out something."

"So it's settled," Gregg said, still in the doorway. When Tanis attempted to pass, he blocked her way. "The business partner to one sister and boyfriend to the other agrees with the arrangement. So all is well."

"Yes, it's settled and Frankie agrees," she replied irritably. "And I don't know why you're being sarcastic. Now, will you please let me go?"

He moved aside slowly, his eyes on her as she passed. Remorse overcame her quite unexpectedly. She had no right to be annoyed with a man who was making such a generous offer to them. Haltingly she told him, "I—I don't know how to thank you, Dr. Barratt."

"I do," Cassandra interposed, and indicated that she wanted Gregg to move nearer. Smiling, he complied. Her arm stretched upward and as he leaned toward her

she held his shoulder and kissed his cheek. "You don't mind, do you?" she asked, uncertain now, as she abandoned the touch of childishness and took on a look of haunting maturity born of the pain she had endured and that still dogged her.

Gregg rested his hands on the arms of her chair and gazed into her round, trusting face. "How could I mind? You know what? I think you're a wonderful person, a young woman in a million. Cheerful in adversity, earnest, honest. One day you'll be the sun in some lucky man's sky." His finger tipped her face, which had drooped. "Oh, yes, you will. And don't frown at me, Cassandra. There are other men in the world besides that young rogue you call your boyfriend."

Tanis turned to stare out of the window, unable to bear the sight of Gregg gazing into Cassandra's bright brown eyes. Each word of praise he had used to her sister, his admiration, had been like the tearing claws of a wild animal on the delicate membranes of her own emotions.

I can't be jealous, she told herself despairingly. *Jealousy implies deeper feelings, like affection, like love!* And she mustn't, couldn't be falling in love with this man...could she?

It had been arranged that Gregg should call for them the following Friday.

"You can stay overnight," he told them. "Get the feel of the place. See how you like it."

Frankie had thought the situation over, he told Tanis as she worked with him. "Once you've settled in the Barratt place, we could try our luck in that area. Better opportunities in that part of the world, bigger houses. We could advertise in the local paper. You could ask your new landlord to whisper our name among his friends."

"You're an opportunist," Tanis accused as they sat

eating their sandwiches in the room of the terrace house they were decorating.

"Yeah," said Frankie, leering at her. "If the lady of the house were out, I'd take the opportunity right now to—"

"Keep off me, Frankie," Tanis warned. "You'll break Cassandra's heart if you don't leave me alone."

"I've got you both where I want you," he said, smiling unpleasantly. "As I said before. So you'll dance to my tune, *Miss Foster*." He attempted to imitate Gregg's way of speaking.

"Leave Dr. Barratt out of this."

"So it's like that." Frankie eyed her and she cursed herself for having put yet another weapon in his hands.

"No, it's not," she lied. "It's just that he's a good man and—"

"You're dead right. He's a *man*. And wasn't he demonstrating it the last time he called on you! Enjoying it, weren't you? Never thought you had it in you."

Tanis crumpled her sandwich paper and threw it at him.

On the day Gregg was due, Frankie commented on Tanis's silence as they worked together on the nearly completed room. Her mind had been occupied almost every minute of every hour with thoughts of Gregg Barratt. His offer of a home had puzzled her.

No matter how often she told herself to accept the fact and be thankful, the question "why?" teased her constantly. Now and then she recalled the way he looked at her, and the thought made her go warm. Nor could she forget how his touch stirred feelings that scared her by their strength, urging her to respond to him in a way that shocked but also excited her.

Yet it was Cassandra with whom he was gentle, whom he praised for her fine character. Not a word of praise for herself had passed his lips. Most of the time he looked at her with mocking, assessing eyes, and con-

demnation was never far away. For what, she wondered. It was she who had waited in the pouring rain for a customer to materialize and buy one of her sister's paintings. It was she, after all, who had brought him into their lives.

Tanis went home early that afternoon. She wanted to look her best for once in Gregg Barratt's presence. *Maybe,* she thought, *if I wear something really feminine, instead of the jeans and T-shirt he usually sees me wearing, he'll look at me as admiringly as he looks at Cassandra.*

Her sister greeted her with the usual sweet smile. It was her words that were a surprise. "Don't do any packing for me. I've decided not to go. It'll be quite sufficient for you to see the place. And don't say 'But, Cassandra....' I'm getting on so well with this painting, I don't want any interruptions."

"I can't leave you just like that," Tanis protested. "Who's going to look after you?"

"I asked Mrs. Yardley. She said she'd be pleased to do all the looking after I wanted."

"Well, if you're sure and she's sure—"

"Ask her. Go on; I know she's in."

Mrs. Yardley was a well-built woman with a decisive, capable manner. Since her husband had died she had not let herself go, dressing smartly even when she stayed at home.

"Enjoy yourself, Miss Foster," she said briskly. "You deserve a break. I've never seen a girl work so hard."

It seemed that Cassandra had not told her of the reason for the weekend away, which, Tanis decided, was probably wise. It might be that Gregg Barratt's house was too much of a stately mansion to be a real home to them.

Downstairs again, Cassandra said, looking at her work from different angles, "Frankie will drop in and

see me if I call him on the phone. We—we haven't been alone together for ages, not really since my stay in hospital.''

The waver in Cassandra's voice, an appeal for reassurance, touched Tanis's heart. "I'm certain he will," she answered. "If he doesn't come before I go, I'll call him and tell him you'll be here on your own.''

Tanis took a quick bath and changed into a closefitting, sleeveless, stone-colored dress. A long-sleeved jacket completed the outfit, while a necklace of individually hand-turned wooden beads added a dramatic and original touch.

Sparingly, thus all the more effectively, she put on makeup, accentuating her almond-shaped brown eyes. Her long lashes and well-marked eyebrows matched perfectly the black of her hair. This she combed until it fell in gently upward-curling layers, clustering around her small ears.

This, she thought, looking at her reflection, was a girl Gregg Barratt had never seen. Would he smile at her with sincerity, without that touch of cynicism that seemed to be ever present when his eyes turned in her direction?

"Great," said Cassandra as her sister entered the room. "It's sure as I can't walk that Gregg will fall for you."

Tanis smiled her thanks, but hid the pain that Cassandra's words created. *You're the one who gets his smiles,* she thought. *I receive his frowns. What basis is that for anything, even for friendship, let alone something deeper?* But she stayed silent, going to the window.

At Cassandra's insistence she gave a description of the drivers of the cars that went by. But even before another car had come into Tanis's view, Cassandra announced, "Ah, now he's coming. I can tell by the sound of the engine.''

"You're right," Tanis exclaimed, and hurried to the

door. The smile with which she greeted him was faint with uncertainty, not lack of welcome, but Gregg seemed to assume it was the latter. His nod was this side of curt and the line of his mouth did not alter. His eyes slid over her, but whether in approval or otherwise, she could not tell.

Tanis followed him into the living room, then returned to her place at the window. He still wore his work suit, although the description hardly did justice to its excellent cut. He answered Cassandra's smile with a warm smile of his own. Envy gained a foothold in her heart, racing up to her eyes. Before Gregg could probe and discover her secret, she put her back to the window and her eyes in shadow. She had, however, misjudged his quickness.

"Feeling quilty," he taunted, "at being caught in the act?" Tanis pretended to be puzzled. "The act of looking out for me. Or—" his cutting glance inspected her dress, which followed uninhibitedly the outline of her figure "—was it someone more important in your life you were expecting?"

"There's no one more important in her life," Cassandra returned firmly, knowing as well as Tanis did the person to whom Gregg referred.

Gregg laughed. "I can hardly deduce from that statement that I come first in your sister's life."

"After me, yes."

"Cassandra Foster," Tanis said, advancing on her and moving her hands in a tearing action, "if you were fighting fit—"

"Tanis likes you," Cassandra went on unrepentantly. "All week she's been like a dog that can't find its home, because you haven't been over. And today she could hardly keep away from that window."

"Thanks, Cassandra." Gregg approached Tanis with lowered head, his eyes lingering on her lips. "So I'm second on your list of favorite people, am I, Miss Foster?"

"First on her list of top ten men," Cassandra prompted chirpily.

Tanis tried to retreat, but the window was behind her. "Look away, young sister," Gregg said over his shoulder, "because I'm going to kiss Miss Tanis Foster into submission."

Cassandra laughed delightedly. "I've put my hands over my eyes," she informed him. "Tell me when it's over."

Then Tanis was in his arms. It was, she thought, like being rescued from a wrecked ship to which she had been clinging for seven long days; so great was the relief that there was no resistance in her. His fist lifted her chin. "Brown eyes," he murmured, "deep as two pools, clear and candid, yet full of secrets. A serious face, intelligent, intriguing and lovely. Where's the artifice that should be there," he was whispering now, "the cunning that knows how to take another girl's man away, even if she is your sister?"

Tanis felt she had been plunged straight back into icy water and was clinging again to the upturned boat. She fought to escape, but his arms were around her so tightly she could hardly breathe. "Making false accusations," she stormed, "sweet-talking me about my looks, then making nasty innuendos about my character."

There was no time to say more. His mouth covered hers and he was pressing her against him, making her more aware of him than she had ever been before. To her dismay, she let herself go, following where he led, willingly parting her lips and feeling the urgency of his desires. If they had been alone, she thought, if there hadn't been an audience. . . .

"Can I look now?" Cassandra's small voice brought Tanis down to earth and loosened Gregg's hold. His growled yes did not mean that Tanis could go free.

"Wow," said Cassandra, "can you kiss, Dr. Barratt!

Do you do that to all the women in your life, or is Tanis number one on *your* list of top ten women?''

"Your young sister is always trying to throw us together," Gregg drawled, evading the question. "Do you think she has a motive?"

Recovering from his shattering kiss, Tanis almost missed Gregg's implication that, in hinting at an attraction between the doctor and herself, Cassandra was snatching Frankie from her clutches. "It's plain you think she has," Tanis hit out. "Also that you agree with her. Well, she's wrong and you're wrong. Now, will you please let me go!"

"At it again?" Frankie stood in the doorway.

Cassandra's back had been to the door. Swinging her chair around, she shrieked, "Frankie, darling!" Her arms came out. "Kiss me the way Dr. Barratt kissed Tanis."

Gregg let Tanis go, but remained at her side.

"Can't oblige, Cassie," Frankie answered, going to her. "I'm way out of his league. Has he got technique!"

"Stop being sarcastic about Dr. Barratt. I think he's wonderful."

Frankie looked from Cassandra to Tanis. "That makes two of you."

"Oh, but I love you best," Cassandra confided as he made for her cheek, but she turned quickly and took the kiss on her mouth.

"I'll practice kissing," he promised carelessly, "then, when you're really better, I'll be able to do it as well as your visitor. Then you can enjoy it as much as your sister did when he kissed her."

"When I'm better?" The radiance had left her face and she looked dubiously at her thin legs. "I don't know when that will be—if ever."

Gregg strolled over to her. "When we first met," he reminded her, "you told me I gave you hope. What's happened to that hope?"

Cassandra's shoulders lifted and dropped. "I guess I've still got it."

"And courage?" She nodded. "Good. Together they're the best medicine of all. Now—" Gregg looked around "—where are the suitcases?"

"There's only one," Tanis informed him. "Cassandra's decided not to come."

"Hope you don't mind," Cassandra apologized. "I'm at a crucial stage in my painting and two days away from it would be very disruptive, if you know what I mean."

"I'm not a creative artist," Gregg answered, smiling, "but I do understand. And before you ask, I don't mind at all, if it's what you want. Who'll look after her?"

He had turned to Tanis. *His smile,* she thought; *it's cooled as usual as if the heat's been turned off.*

Cassandra answered. "Mrs. Yardley upstairs. She was a nurse, but she's retired now. Frankie will come and see me, too." Her hand extended toward him. "Won't you?"

"If you want—I mean, of course, Cassie." Frankie had turned red at his near blunder. Cassandra, however, had not missed the casual attitude, despite his effort to cover it.

Frowning in a touching bewilderment, she asked, "Don't you want to see me? Okay—" her shoulders rose and fell "—I don't care, not one bit."

Knowing Gregg Barratt's eyes were on him, he went quickly to Cassandra's side. "Honey, of course I want to." He ruffled her hair, then, realizing at once that it was too brotherly an action, bent to tilt her chin, kissing her lips. Duty done, Tanis thought acidly, then found Frankie was looking at her. And also that Gregg was looking at Frankie looking at her.

Her eyes sought Gregg's, willing them her way; then she wished she hadn't. A glacier, she thought, would have been warm compared with Gregg's cold gaze.

THE APPROACH TO GREGG BARRATT'S HOUSE was down a
narrow road. The long, wide car brushed the hedges. If
another vehicle had appeared, it could not have passed.

Apprehensive at Gregg's apparent lack of concern as
he drove along the road, Tanis was moved to ask, "I
suppose this goes only to your house?" He nodded and
her smile was part relief, part provocation. "That ex-
plains your lord-of-the-manor attitude. Nothing, but
nothing, can take precedence over the privileged owner
of stately home and surrounding estate."

A lightning-fast turn of the head brought his flicking
glance to sting her face. Then he smiled at the road
ahead, saying sardonically, "I've had many things from
my women guests, but never undiluted impudence. It
makes a change." He turned the wheel to the left. "But
if you're expecting a stately home, you're in for a disap-
pointment."

The car passed through two wide-open ironwork
gates. It seemed he had been expected. The driveway to
the front entrance was circular, making for easy approach and exit.

"All the same, it's a lovely-looking house," Tanis
commented. "Just look at those grouped chimneys and
the gables and the deep red brick." The car came to a
stop outside an archway in which was recessed a heavy
wooden door. Her eyes skimmed the facade of the
building, noting the small windows. "It's almost asking
to be painted."

Gregg laughed and leaned back, resting his arm along
the top of her seat. "Touting for business? Does your
decorative eye see scope for your talents?"

Tanis smiled. "I didn't mean it that way, but I'd take
a guess it's going to suffer structurally before long
unless something's done to stop the deterioration of the
woodwork." After a pause she said, "It's just as if it's
reaching out its arms." Her serious brown eyes sought
his. "I think it's welcoming you home."

He met her gaze steadily and she felt her heartbeats quicken. This man had only to look at her and her reflexes responded. "Are you sure," he queried, "it's not you it's welcoming?"

Her dark hair lifted and swung as she contemplated the house again. "Maybe it is," she conceded. "Yes, I think you're right. Even without going inside, I've got a feeling—"

"A good feeling?"

Tanis nodded, then turned to smile at him again.

His eyes studied her face. "I'm glad," he replied, but he did not return her smile.

A man appeared in the archway and walked toward the car. Gregg greeted him, then helped Tanis from the car. The man lifted her suitcase and shoulder bag from the trunk. "Is that all, Dr. Barratt?" he asked respectfully.

Gregg nodded. "An unusual guest, George. She obviously believes in traveling light. I'll take a guess the case contains one toothbrush and nothing else."

"You've forgotten the toothpaste," Tanis prompted with an impish flash of her eyes. "And I do wear a nightdress when I go to bed."

Gregg and his employee exchanged glances and Gregg laughed loudly. "Forewarned is forearmed," he drawled, and smiled at the resulting blush. "Quits, Miss Foster?" He seemed to enjoy the sparks of anger that her eyes spat out.

The entrance hall into which Tanis stepped was large with wood-paneled walls. A curving staircase led upward while daylight shone through the windows, some of which, Tanis estimated, had probably been added at a later date.

A woman, slightly built with graying hair, came through one of the doors that opened off the entrance hall. Tanis returned her smile of welcome.

"I'm Mrs. Casey," the woman introduced herself,

"Dr. Barratt's housekeeper. George—you've already seen him—is my husband. Enjoy your stay...Miss Foster, isn't it? I've heard about your sister—such a pity. Never mind; Dr. Barratt will find a way of having her on her feet again. He'll move heaven and earth, you can be sure of that."

"Tanis. In here." Gregg's voice, slightly autocratic, summoned her. Mrs. Casey indicated the room and Tanis entered, joining her host at the window.

"What beautiful gardens," she exclaimed. Her eyes swept the greenery, the shrubs and rose bushes. "That view, those trees, everything coming into bud." She recalled the view from the window of their own home. "No traffic noise," she commented, half to herself, "just peace and quiet."

Lifting her head, she found his eyes on her face. Awareness stirred inside her. At his slightly mocking smile it strengthened like a stroking breeze growing into a roughening wind. The effect of this man on her senses was becoming alarming.

"So—" he seemed amused "—my home has passed the censor?"

Smiling, she nodded.

He persisted, "Outside you said you felt the place was reaching out its arms. Can you now feel it sweeping you into them?"

Tanis looked around as if considering his probing question, although she knew the answer already. "I've seen only a very small part," she prevaricated. "I'll need to look at every part of the place before I can arrive at a conclusion."

His smile was cool at her reply. "Do you have to look at every part of everything—everyone—before you come to a conclusion about whether or not you approve of the arms that might be holding you?"

"If you insist on becoming personal, as I think you are, well, I can't deny ever having been in any other

man's arms but yours." She was frowning now at the view she had praised. "Cassandra did tell you I'd had boyfriends, but—believe it or not—I haven't been so deeply involved with any of them that I've ever seen 'every part' of them."

"Never deeply involved?" His skeptical tone brought angry color to her cheeks.

"If you're now implying I'm having an affair with Frank Anderson behind Cassandra's back, then you're wrong, *wrong*, Dr. Barratt."

Eyebrows lifted cynically, but all he said was, "I think it's time you called me Gregg, Tanis."

"It won't be easy. I call my friends by their first names, but—"

"You don't look on me as a friend?"

Tanis gave him a skimming look. Shoulders so broad they seemed strong enough to bear the weight of her troubles as well as his own; arms so powerful she wanted to lose herself in them; a chin so firm and a jaw so thrusting they made "obstinacy" his second name. Not to mention a mouth that could crash through a woman's barriers of resistance, no matter how high she built them.... Could she call this man a *friend*?

CHAPTER FOUR

"NO?" GREGG ASKED, eyebrows raised, eyes keen and knowing.

It seemed he had been following the ski trail of her thoughts and had even overtaken her. He was smiling his enigmatic smile.

"No." He nodded once, and she went on, "But I'll try. To call you Gregg, I mean."

"How do you think of me? As Dr. Barratt? Or don't you think of me?"

Tanis cursed the giveaway color. "I think of you... as Gregg."

"Good. So that should help, shouldn't it."

If I look at him now, she thought, *he'll be smiling sarcastically.* So she resumed her scanning of the view.

Mrs. Casey said from the door, "Dinner in half an hour, Dr. Barratt?" He nodded. To Tanis she said, "When you're ready I'll show you to your room."

Tanis thanked her and the woman left them. "Gregg?" The name sounded too familiar to be addressed to such a man, whose status demanded the highest respect. All the same she repeated, "Gregg? Do you dress for dinner? I mean, do you insist on formality?"

His smile in response warmed her like the sun in the tropics. This, she thought, basking in it for the short time it was hers, was how he smiled at Cassandra. The charm radiated by the look in his fascinatingly colored eyes was breath-catching, and for a moment she found it hard to speak. How good it would be, she reflected, if

she were on the receiving end of that all-enveloping charm for the rest of her life.

"How would you feel if I said yes?"

She met his amused look squarely. "At home we call it our evening meal, or tea, or supper. Sometimes I don't bother to change out of my jeans and T-shirt. Cassandra just wears what she's worn all day. That's how informal we are."

"There's no need to be on the defensive with me, my beautiful Tanis." His finger curled under her chin, lifting her face. "What are you afraid of—that you and your sister will find yourselves fitting into my way of life like a key in the wrong keyhole?"

"Yes." Her lower lip pouted a little. It was an involuntary action, denoting rebellion, but Gregg plainly saw it as an invitation he could not resist.

His mouth lowered and he placed two light kisses on the startled lips that parted to receive his. Then he gazed down at her and she gazed back, eyes wide and wondering. *I'm waiting for more,* she thought with dismay, and jerked free of his supporting hand.

He smiled faintly and she wished she could read his thoughts as he seemed able to read hers. "To me you look fine as you are. Wherever my profession might place me on the social scale, Tanis, under my skin I'm just an uncomplicated male."

Her sideways look was half-hidden by her long lashes, and her mouth curved teasingly. "You're just a simple guy at heart."

"As your contemporaries would say."

Her face lifted to his. "I don't believe you."

He took her statement as a challenge, and his hand caught her arm.

"Dr. Barratt—" Mrs. Casey stood at the door "—shall I show Miss Foster to her room now?"

"Don't provoke me again, witch, or you might regret

it,'' Gregg said softly as they followed the housekeeper upstairs.

The room to which Mrs. Casey took Tanis was, she explained, next to the one that her sister would have if they did come and live there. Tanis thanked her and she said, "If you'll excuse me now, I'll be serving dinner."

Tanis glanced up at the ceiling and her professional eye noted the dulling white of the paintwork. The walls, too, were in need of decoration.

"Making an estimate of the cost of your services?" Gregg leaned, arms folded, against the doorway.

"Yes." Tanis smiled widely. "It'll cost you millions."

Gregg pretended to mop his brow. "I knew the place was in a bad way decoratively, but I didn't think it would bankrupt me to have it put right."

Her long lashes lowered. "I might, just might, lower the price for you."

Slowly, hands in pockets with the jacket draped over them, he approached her. "A beautiful girl, a bed, a price—and a man willing to accept the price *without* its being lowered." Tanis retreated backward toward the window. Gregg followed, gripping her arms and pressing her painfully against the ridge of the windowsill.

"You know I didn't mean that," she protested, pressing with all her strength away from the sill, only to find herself pressed instead—and much more alarmingly— against his body.

Seeing her predicament, Gregg smiled, his lids halflowered as he looked at her. "A choice of two evils," he said with a touch of malice. "If you don't like the feel of me, push yourself back and get hurt."

With her palms against his chest, she gazed up at him. Her heart pounded at the feel of his legs in contact with hers, the hardness of his hips, his breath on her face. "Whatever I do," she whispered, "I'll get hurt." And she didn't care if he guessed her meaning.

He was following her mental footsteps again. "Meaning I'll hurt you physically...or emotionally?"

His eyes were hypnotizing her and she answered, "Both, Gregg." She was committing herself too far, enmeshing herself in his dragnet, and once there she would never escape. Her face turned away. "I'm sorry. Forget it. Don't let it bother you."

The stroke of a kiss made the skin of her cheek come alive. Her head turned back and his mouth sketched a tingling line to settle on her protesting lips. In no time at all the line of her body was softening to mold with his.

Her hands found his shoulders and clung with a fierceness all their own, as if they had sensed the stability and security for which their owner had unconsciously been seeking ever since she had been forced by circumstances to take on the responsibility of caring for an invalid sister.

The tap on the door had her languor-limp muscles tensing, her hands pushing instead of pulling. But her mouth still had not been released from his searching exploration, and the feelings its thoroughness had aroused were still not quelled, even when Mrs. Casey called, "Dr. Barratt, will you and Miss Foster please come down to dinner?"

Slowly the pressure eased and his lips lifted to move in answering acknowledgement. The housekeeper's steps sounded disapproving as they took her away, but that did nothing to dull the gleam in Gregg's eyes.

He glanced at the bed and remarked softly, "If a man took you there with him, he'd know the greatest satisfaction of body and the most pleasurable easing of mind a woman could ever give him."

The picture his words flashed before her eyes created a peculiar weakness in her legs and the strangest desire to put her arms around his body. Since it was necessary at all costs to hide her feelings, she fenced, "Are you paying me a compliment?"

"You know damned well I am." His sharp retort threw her, but only for a moment.

"Not necessarily," she came back. "You could be placing me in a . . . very different category of woman."

His eyes signaled danger. "Don't try my restraint too far. The suggestion came from you. It originated in your mind. Does it imply you'd like me to treat you as a professional sleep-around? Payment in cash, of course."

The heat in her cheeks spread downward and she turned away. "I'm sorry. I asked for that."

"You asked for more than that, believe me. Come on, let's eat."

To Tanis's surprise, the atmosphere over the meal was relaxed. The conversation was mainly about the business she ran with her partner.

"How did it happen," Gregg asked after coffee as they sat on the couch in the living room, "that a girl with your assets, mental as well as physical, became involved in interior decorating?"

Tanis shrugged. "Since my father died, I was the one in the family who decorated the house."

"Outside as well as in?" He leaned back, his eyes on her profile.

With difficulty Tanis kept her face averted, which meant that he continued to enjoy his contemplation of her straight, neat nose, the delicate sweep of her jaw, the inviting, natural pout of her lips.

"Of course." Her head turned sharply. "I've told you I'm not afraid of climbing ladders, nor of heights."

"Reason prevailing over emotion, as I would have guessed." His glance was lazy.

"Yes," she retorted, "intellect over feeling. It's something I've always cultivated."

"That I can well believe." His eyes glinted at her attempt at sarcasm. "And intellect you have in plenty. What a blend—beauty plus intelligence! No wonder

your business partner reacts the way he does when you're around.''

Tanis took a breath to deny the implication his statement held, but snapped her lips shut again. What was the use, she asked herself. He would never believe her, especially as he had seen with his own eyes the way Frankie behaved toward her, even in front of the girl whose boyfriend he was supposed to be.

On impulse she turned toward him. "You're a doctor, Gregg. When Frankie looks at me in that certain way, when he holds my hand so that everyone can see, as he did the other day, what would you advise me to do? Lift his hand to my mouth and bite it? Knowing him, he'd probably take it as a come-on signal. Or give him a purring look, like a stricken kitten, which he'd also take as encouragement? Whichever I did, the result would be the same, wouldn't it? You should know. I mean, you're a man as well as a doctor. You told me. I just couldn't win, could I? Whatever I did I'd be a boyfriend snatcher in your eyes.''

He saw her hurt, puzzled look and leaned forward, hands clasped. "You don't exactly push him away.''

If she told him the truth—that she was afraid he'd leave her and start a decorating business of his own, thus causing a financial upheaval for her because she would be lost for work without him, and a devasting emotional upheaval for Cassandra—would he believe her? That answer was no, so she didn't even try.

She lifted her shoulders and sighed. "All right, so I don't push him away.''

His head came around, eyes heavy with knowledge of women's ways and their dishonesty. A silent answer and also an accusation—and it brought her to her feet. "I need my sleep, Gregg.'' Her smile bore an assumed weariness, and it convinced him.

Outside her room, his eyes ran over her. Her upward gaze challenged unconsciously. If he was going to kiss

her. . . . His mouth curved slightly as if he had guessed her thoughts.

"Sleep well, Tanis," was all he said.

WAKING EARLY THE NEXT MORNING, Tanis lay and listened to the country silence. The sun's rays grew stronger, probing a way into the room through the gap in the heavy curtains. The fervor of the morning birdsong had her bare feet tiptoeing over the rugs to let the sunshine in. Her heart and hope rose with the skylarks into a clear blue sky.

After breakfast Gregg took Tanis on a tour of the house. She lost count of the number of bedrooms. He explained his plans for alterations, the installation of bathrooms en suite with some of the bedrooms.

"Where are you planning to hang Cassandra's paintings?" Tanis asked as they wandered around.

"They're stored away at present. When the renovations are complete, in the main living rooms." Pleased, Tanis nodded.

Downstairs again, Gregg asked, "Well, what's your verdict?"

"Of the state of the place?" He nodded. She smiled widely. "It badly needs the attentions of first-class interior decorators."

His smile was sarcastic. "Name of Foster and Anderson?"

"But of course. All others are inferior."

His fisted hand brushed her chin. "Cheeky imp. For your impudence, you and your partner have won the job."

Her eyes glowed. "You mean that?"

"I do. You want me to sign a contract?"

She pretended to consider, putting her head on one side. "I think I can take your word for it—as the gentleman you are."

He approached her slowly, hands in pockets pushing

his V-necked sweater into folds. "How many times have I kissed you? Was I a gentleman then?" His eyes were smiling.

Her lips were just a little tremulous as she returned his warm glance. "Yes, because you...knew when to stop."

"Don't count on that lasting, Tanis." He towered over her, close enough to touch her but plainly having no intention of doing so. Which, she acknowledged deep down, riled her somewhat. "Most times we had an audience, watching or listening. Scratch my skin and you'll find the male in me. Score my flesh and draw blood and you'll find an animal leaping at your throat."

Her eyes held his boldly, her mouth curved, her hands moved upward. Eight fingers curved stiffly and eight nails ran lightly down his cheek. His hands whipped free of the pockets, seizing her wrists, jerking them to her sides.

"After that calculated little piece of provocation, don't ask me to believe you're inviolate."

She had meant him to laugh, but his anger was bruising, frightening. "I've never asked you to believe anything about me," she fenced.

"Not even to accept that Frank Anderson is nothing more to you than your partner in business?"

Cursing the heat that warmed her cheeks, she could only look down, seeing as she did so the hard hips of him, the strong legs that must have supported him through many hours of demanding, exhausting work in the operating room. It reminded her of what had been so easy to forget since she had been under his roof as his guest, being treated with the courtesy and attention meted out, no doubt, to all his visitors: his profession and status.

Her wrists twisted free and she rubbed them, her head lifting. "Yes, I do expect you to believe that. What I did to you just now was only meant as fun."

"If it's fun you want, I can give you plenty. There's no need to get it from Cassandra's boyfriend."

Anger fired her eyes. Her hand swung, but he did not flinch. The hand dropped unused to her side and she turned away. "You'd better take me home."

Hands resting on her shoulders stopped her move to the door. "I've made plans. This afternoon I'll show you the area. This evening we're dining out."

Fingers touched her neck, stroking, soothing. Surgeon though he was, his hands were healing without incision, healing her temper, mending her mood, assuaging the pain his own accusations caused.

She shivered and could not hide it, leaning back on him, head to his chest, eyes fluttering closed. To him she must have looked a picture of contentment, but, clever though he was, he could not see the storm of feeling brewing deep inside her body. Her pulses raced, her heart cried in silent anguish, *why did it have to be you I fell in love with?*

"HAVE I TOLD YOU how beautiful you look?" They were standing in the wood-paneled entrance hall, facing each other. "That dress enhances everything about you."

Tanis did not know whether his praise was small talk or meant sincerely, but her eyes shone all the same. "I'm glad you like the dress."

"I like the girl in it more."

Like—so neutral, so impartial that Tanis despaired, but her smile stayed in place. She knew the dress did things for her. In the shop it had taken her nearly an hour to decide on it, trying the assistant's patience to the limit. It was something she had never done before and afterward, seeing the sales clerk's tiredness, vowed never to do again.

The background color was a midnight blue, scattered with tiny white floral motifs. The sleeves reached her wrists and the wraparound top outlined her rounded

shape, its neckline plunging to cross and meet at the small waist. The skirt, in contrast, was tiered and hung full and feminine to the toe-touching hemline.

"Did you bring a wrap?"

Solemnly she shook her head. "I'm afraid my past boyfriends haven't been rich enough to buy me a fur stole."

His eyes flashed, warning of danger. "Don't play with me, Tanis. Unless you're ready for the consequences?"

The answer, *yes, oh, yes,* almost forced itself from her lips. Instead she turned away, saying flatly, "I'll wear my coat."

It was a restaurant that coaxed its patrons into forgetting their cares. It made Gregg look at Tanis with lazy eyes. Tanis responded with a seductive smile and lowered lashes. Music played softly, sensuously. Multicolored lights were strung across the ceiling; lanterns shed red, lemon and peacock blue from wooden pillars.

Vines had been trained to trail across the ceiling from sturdy twining treelike trunks in shaded corners. Tanis moved a spoon, making the brilliantly colored reflections move and change shape. She glanced outside and a long way into the distance; streetlights, echoing those across the ceiling, climbed hills and descended them.

The waiter came and their order was discussed and decided upon. A jug was placed on their table and Gregg, without asking, poured water into Tanis's glass. She thanked him and lifted the glass high, watching the dancing lights through it. She put the glass to her lips.

"It's like drinking colored bubbles," she commented.

"And it's giving a multicolored glitter to your eyes," Gregg added. "Twenty-four hours here and you're already a different girl."

He leaned back, relaxed and handsome, and his smile tugged at her heartstrings. His arm hung loosely over the back of his chair. "You're a beautiful woman," he said quietly.

Tanis hoped the lowered lighting would hide the color his praise created in her cheeks. "Your world must be full of beautiful women."

"Must it? Why?"

A reasonable question, but she stammered over the answer. Her shoulders lifted and fell. "You—you must attract them the way a mountain attracts climbers."

His head went back in laughter. "So I'm a mountain now?"

Yes, she wanted to whisper, *an unconquerable one. If I lived here it would be torment seeing you almost every day, loving you yet having to keep my distance.*

He still required an answer, and she said in a mock-dramatic voice, "A towering one, unclimbable, with a sheer face on every side." Her brown eyes danced. "Remote and snowcapped and—and cold."

He was leaning toward her at that. "Cold? I'd like to show you just how cold." His eyes glittered like the snow she had just talked about.

Her reply was to look away, outside at the darkness broken by the strings of yellow streetlights. There was a pause during which he leaned back again.

Then the meal was served. The food was good, the wine Gregg had ordered pleasing to the palate. All the time they talked, of Gregg's work and Tanis's childhood. Over coffee they grew silent, and Tanis realized how much she had enjoyed the evening with Gregg.

He broke the silence, asking, "You think Cassandra will like living here?"

Her dark head swung around to him. "She'd love it. It would appeal to the artist in her, to her yearning for good living and lush greenery."

"What about her sister?"

The question confused her for a second, then she laughed. "Me. Oh, I don't know." He did not speak. She drew circles on the white tablecloth. "It's so different. The environment, the neighborhood." *I'm*

lying, she scolded herself. *I'd love it here.* "What would I do in my spare time? I—I might just get bored." His gaze was hard, enigmatic. "I—I suppose I could help the housekeeper." His look did not alter, and she frowned. "No, I suppose I couldn't."

"Come on." He spoke at last. "Time we were leaving."

The journey back was silent except for the passing cars. When they entered the driveway and braked by the entrance door, the quietness seeped into Tanis's body. Her head went back and her eyes closed at the peace. Peace to be beside him, peace to hear his breathing... turmoil when he leaned across her to replace her coat, which had slipped from her shoulders.

If the touch of him did this to her, how could she hide her feelings if she came to live here?

It was late and the housekeeper and her husband had gone to bed. Gregg followed Tanis up the stairs. Outside her room, she paused. "Thank you and good night," she said.

His hands found her shoulders, turned her and urged her inside the room. It seemed he was prepared to stay and talk. Or—her large eyes searched his—had he something else in mind?

His hands fastened around her arms. She felt the firm strength of them and knew that if he ever had to attend her medically she would have total trust in him. His fingers began to slide up to her throat, and she let them be. His thumbs tipped back her head and his eyes lingered on her every feature. Her breath struggled from her lungs, her hands clutched at bunches of her skirt.

His palms moved down, down to the full shape of her, finding at last her breasts and cupping them, and she let him. His head lowered, his lips settling on the deep point of her neckline. His dark head so near, his hands in such exquisite possession, made her want to bury her fingers in the thickness of his hair, to put her

cheek against it, to whisper to him to make love to her.

Her hands moved at last, to find his shoulders. As he straightened, still holding her, her hands gripped the breadth of him. If she spoke the words "I want you, Gregg. I've been foolish enough to fall in love with you," would he treat her statement with contempt, pushing her away?

"Why are you looking so worried?" he asked softly. "I know exactly how to please a woman."

Her mouth had grown dry. "With—with the experience you must have, I'm—I'm not surprised."

"Sarcastic, bright eyes?"

"I'm sure it's the truth."

"I'm warm-blooded, so what did you expect?"

The words stung and activated her hands into pulling at his to free her body from his maddeningly potent touch. He allowed her to remove his hands, then swung them around so that her wrists were in his grasp. He lifted them toward the light, looking at her fingertips.

Quickly she clenched her hands. "I can't help my broken nails," she defended herself. "I work hard for my living. You can't paint woodwork and walls with gloves on."

"Who said a word?" It was a mild rebuke. "Do you really believe I'd think any the worse of you for bearing the scars inflicted by your job? What kind of a man do you think I am?"

"A mountain," she returned, attempting a smile.

"Ah, yes. And, like a mountain summit—" his eyes narrowed with remembrance "—cold. *Cold*. I'll show you how cold!"

In his arms was sanctuary, security and strength. There was also a mounting pleasure as his mouth took hers into his temporary keeping, searching it for hidden sweetness, drawing from her a response that, no matter how much she gave, did not seem to satisfy his needs.

She was excited by his thighs, the feel of his legs

touching hers, his hand in her hair. Then that hand was moving to find the swelling femininity, caressing her skin into exquisite sensitivity, moving tantalizingly in arousal and bringing to her body a weakness that carried her to the brink of surrender. Reason struggled weakly to impose its will. Give to this man what he was plainly wanting? When he already thought she was snatching Cassandra's boyfriend, even while Cassandra sat and watched?

He must have felt her change of mood. He eased away, losing contact and, to her passion-warmed eyes, seeming strangely detached. All he revealed to her slightly shocked gaze was a quickened breathing that was swiftly under control, and a crumpled jacket that was soon straightened.

"Yes," she said, her voice shaking just a little, "have you got experience!" Had she made her voice lilt enough, as if it were to her a lighthearted interlude? It seemed she had, judging by the angry movement of his jaw.

"Resulting partly, as you said, from experience, and partly from a textbook knowledge of a woman's anatomy." After the lovemaking, his voice grated unbearably.

"You make it sound so horribly clinical," she accused, still feeling bruised from his kisses, "when it should be warm, spontaneous and—and infused with love."

His smile was not the result of amusement, and certainly not love. "I'd make it easy. I'd tell you at the start, 'Tanis, I love you.'"

"No deal," she whispered, her face white, her sparkle entirely gone. "You wouldn't mean it."

He stood there, tall, distinguished—and entirely out of reach. He stretched out a hand and with a flick of his fingers and the faintest curl to his lips pulled the neckline of her dress back into place.

SUNDAY BROUGHT THE SAME BRIGHT MORNING SUN, which for spring was surprisingly warm. Tanis breakfasted alone, Gregg having apparently risen earlier and gone out.

There was a sense of anticlimax in sitting on her own at the dining-room table, waiting to be served by the housekeeper. Managing a smile when Mrs. Casey entered, Tanis commented brightly on how appetizing the food looked. The housekeeper nodded, said, "Drink your orange juice, dear," and whisked out.

Her appetite was good, and Mrs. Casey, collecting the dishes, said it must have been the country air. The coffee, freshly made, tasted excellent, too, and Tanis helped herself to two cups.

"Alone and lonely. An unhappy combination." The dry voice came from behind. Tanis swung around to see Gregg framed in the doorway to the garden, both doors having been fixed open. He strolled in and stood behind his own chair, his hands in his pockets, his dark blue shirt partly unbuttoned, the close-fitting slacks possessing a fresh look as though Mrs. Casey made sure they were always clean, pressed and ready for wear.

The housekeeper entered. "Finished, Miss Foster?" she asked. "Good. When you've gone I'll clear away." She bustled back to the kitchen.

"Come on," Gregg ordered, holding out his hand. Without hesitation Tanis took it and walked happily by his side as they went through the doors.

They spent the morning in the gardens. There was a lily pond shaped like a half-moon, with a small fountain causing ripples and spray. There were lawns as green as emerald and with the look of velvet. There was a walled garden full of the promise of roses to come. Bright spring flowers colored the borders and the bench seats were kept brightly varnished.

Behind a hedge was an area that, Gregg explained, he intended to convert into a swimming pool. He looked at

the large rectangular area that at present was rough with weeds and stones. His eyes were distant, as though even at that moment he was picturing the finished product, gleaming blue-tinted water, the area around the pool set with matching tiles.

"It will be fine for Cassandra when you both come to live here."

"It wouldn't hurt Cassie to swim?"

"After further treatment, which—" he looked at her "—you must realize she needs—" Tanis nodded "—it will help to strengthen her muscles."

"It would be wonderful for her, if—" his eyes had not moved from her face "—when and if we have saved up enough money." She added, "Your buying all those paintings helped us so much, Gregg. There's still quite a lot more money needed, but I'm determined to get it somehow."

He gazed again at the untouched expanse of earth and she followed his eyes. She found she could almost see that pool, too—hear the laughter, the splashing, the cries of pure happiness from a newly liberated Cassandra.

There was one thing wrong with that vision of the future. She, Tanis, was not there.

CHAPTER FIVE

THE HOUSEKEEPER carried the morning coffee into the garden. Gregg had unfolded a garden chair for Tanis. Head back, she relaxed, loving the caress of the spring sunshine.

Gregg lay on a rug on the grass. His hands cushioned his head and he watched the progress of the white cumulus clouds moving majestically across the sky. When the housekeeper came to collect the tray, Gregg said, "Thanks, Mrs. Casey," without moving his position.

He said suddenly to Tanis, "Come down here."

"No, thank you. This chair's too comfortable to leave."

"Stop behaving like the gracious lady of the house. Come down to earth, hard earth. It's better for your back."

Tanis sat upright. "I'm certainly not acting the gracious lady!"

"Prove it," he taunted. His hand fastened onto her ankle. His touch was so disturbing that a shock ran through her leg. She bent down to prize away his hand, but found herself being pulled mercilessly toward him, leg first.

"No!" she shrieked. "If I hit the ground from this chair, I'll hurt my spine. You should know that."

"Then come down."

There was no other choice. She joined him on the rug.

"I wouldn't have pulled you far enough to damage you, anyway," he stated, turning and smiling into her

scarlet face. His goading words made her dive away from him, but his grip on her arm was too hard to allow her to escape. "Now that I've got you where I want you," he said, "you're staying."

They were lying face to face and Tanis longed to run her fingertips over the dark shadow around his chin and cheeks. Instead her eyes followed the path and she heard him say, "Come on, touch me." She smiled without complying. He took her hand and put it against his face. "Ask the inevitable question." His eyes sparked a challenge. "'Haven't you forgotten to shave?' The answer's no, I haven't—forgotten or shaved. This being the weekend, and having a woman to keep me company, I thought I'd turn primitive man and start returning to my natural state."

"Primitive man," she provoked laughingly. "What an exciting thought!"

His eyes glinted at the challenge and Tanis laughed again. She passed her hand over the black stubble, then ran a finger along the groove from mouth to nose, moving finally to trace the thick arch of his left eyebrow. The mere act of touching him so intimately made her heart spin.

There was a throbbing in her fingertips where they made contact with his skin. When her other hand went to the dark curling growth of hair on his chest, sliding down until yet another button of his shirt came open, he gripped her wrist and used it to jerk her against him.

"Enough's as much as a man can stand," he growled. "I said touch me, not seduce me. Didn't you realize what you were doing?"

"No," she answered, but her smile said yes.

He rolled on top of her and pinned her arms and wrists above her head. His mouth explored hers yet again, as if with each excursion he found new tastes to delight him. It was agony feeling the pressure of him,

yet having to hold herself back from responding in the way her love for him urged her to do.

"Gregg, my dear! Are you so frustrated you couldn't wait for my arrival?"

Gregg's tautened limbs had eased in seconds, but his mouth still held Tanis's in bondage. When he finally released her lips, the gasp she would have given at the intrusion upon their private world had died an unnatural death. So, she thought, had her heart. The Keep Out: Private Property note in the female voice had been too clear to be misunderstood.

The woman who had spoken wore a floral sun top and tight white trousers. Her bared shoulders were faintly freckled, as was her face under the perfectly groomed auburn hair. Her figure was showy—there was, Tanis thought, still stunned and unbelieving, no other word for it. The newcomer did not look Gregg Barratt's type at all. It seemed, however, that she *was* his—and, moreover, considered him hers.

Whether Gregg agreed with his visitor's attitude of possession was more difficult to determine, since he now rested back on his elbows and appeared to have no intention of rising in polite, let alone pleased, greeting.

"I expected you for dinner, not lunch," he said, eyeing the woman in a way that made Tanis want to hit out at him. "I thought you were on duty this afternoon."

"Things were slack. My deputy agreed to do my stint in the ward."

Which meant, Tanis guessed, that she was a nurse. Tanis stood, trying in vain to brush her T-shirt free of creases. They were imprinted into the fabric by wear, and not only by the weight of Gregg's body.

The visitor clearly did not consider this to be the case, as the contempt with which she eyed Tanis's clothes revealed. When the woman's detailed examination reached her apparent rival's face, the watered-down brown of her eyes paled even more with a stifled fury.

Gregg glanced from one to the other. He was smiling and completely good-humoured. "Beautiful, isn't she, Lola?" His lazy eyes switched to a slow contemplation of Tanis. "She's got everything, plus intelligence." He got to his feet and hooked his thumbs into the belt around his waist. "The only thing she won't do...yet—" his eyes went from Tanis to the woman called Lola, then back to Tanis "—is surrender her virginity. However—" he smiled at Tanis's swift angry breath "—I'm working on it."

"Have your fun before we're married, darling," Lola advised, going to him. "After that I promise I'm going to keep you tied to me for life." Her arm linked through Gregg's and she gazed up at him.

"Just as you did your almost ex-husband?"

Lola snatched her arm away. "You're a swine, Gregg Barratt. You know damned well why my husband found another woman. Because of the hours I work, darling—" she stared winsomely into his face "—beside you in the operating room."

He looked easily back at her and his smile was threaded with cynicism. His visitor looked as if she would like to slap his face. His eyes dared her to do just that and she appeared to be silently but unquestionably crushed.

Her anger, however, needed to be vented on someone. She swung to Tanis, who was smoothing back her hair. "And where did you find that lovely specimen?" Her glare proclaimed the insincerity of her description.

"Would you believe me if I told you selling paintings at a roadside stand in the pouring rain?"

"I'd believe you," Lola sneered.

"How *could* you?" Tanis accused staring at Gregg.

"My sweet, it's the truth," Gregg answered unperturbed.

Tanis swung around and wandered away. Gregg did not follow. She found the lily pond and did not care that

the fountain made splashes on her jeans. They were old anyway, she reasoned.

In that moment she became convinced that, no matter how much she longed for circumstances to be different, Gregg Barratt would never belong to her.

"WELL?" The question was asked in a reasonable tone, but even so Tanis could not let her own reason answer. Her emotions were in a turmoil and would not be tamed.

"Why didn't you tell me you were engaged to be married?"

"Am I? That's news to me."

"That woman, Lola—she said so."

"Did she? I only heard her say 'before we're married.' Nothing about an engagement."

"You're splitting hairs."

"And your jealousy is showing."

They were standing in the lounge, and Gregg had a half-empty beer glass in his hand.

"Jealous?" Tanis exclaimed in a tone that was convincingly incredulous. Somehow she had to distract him from that line of thought, since it would inevitably lead him to the truth—that she was indeed jealous, unbearably so. "If—if anybody's jealous," she observed, on the defensive, "it's your medical colleague." She could not bring herself to call the woman by her name.

"Lola? Why should she be jealous?"

Which could only mean, Tanis thought despairingly, that he had indeed only been having his fun with her and that Lola therefore had nothing to worry about.

"Wouldn't you be jealous," she persisted all the same, "if you'd found the woman you love lying entwined in the arms of another man?"

He appeared to consider the question and in doing so let his gaze wander all over her. It was as though in his imagination he was again in physical contact with the

curves and inviting softness of her body, touching places he had touched before.

So intense was his regard, Tanis almost felt his arms around her, the pressure of him pinning her to the ground; felt the same surging response of her reflexes, the rekindling of her desire. Coloring deeply at her own reactions, she turned away, hoping to hide from him the longings his scrutiny had aroused.

"Yes," he answered at last, and she knew she was not imagining the hard note in his voice, "I'd be filled with a jealousy so primitive I'd want to tear the man—and the woman—limb from limb."

A shiver took hold of her at the viciousness of his reply. "Metaphorically," she added weakly. "Not in reality?" Her voice had lifted in a question, but he had not replied.

IT WAS AFTER LUNCH and Gregg was driving Tanis home. She was suffering acutely from a sense of anticlimax. At least, that was what she told herself. The feeling of despondency had to be explained away somehow.

"You're quiet."

"Sorry," she replied, unaware of the weariness in her voice.

He flicked her a look. What had he seen, she wondered, with those cool, keenly professional eyes?

"Have you worked out your arrangements for renting your apartment and packing your things?"

"It may take a while to find the right kind of tenant."

"If necessary, I should be able to find someone in need of a home."

Tanis thanked him and felt that everything was falling into place—whether she wanted it to or not.

"Tanis?" Cassandra called excitedly as they entered the house. "Oh, Tanis—" she looked up at her sister,

her face full of expectation "—tell me what you think. Will we be happy there?"

Tanis kissed her sister's cheek, but Cassandra was too impatient for such a greeting. Then she saw Gregg. "You've brought him in, so it must be all right! Gregg, it's so good to see you. I've painted and painted until I've almost run out of supplies. You should see the masterpieces I've produced! I've spent the whole weekend—"

"Frankie?" Tanis asked.

"Frankie? He came to see me." Her voice had gone as colorless as her cheeks. "Once, for a few minutes." Cassandra dragged in a breath. Her arms went out. "Gregg, oh, Gregg." He bent down and she clutched at him around the neck. "Find a way to make me better. Get me on my feet somehow, as I used to be; then Frankie will love me again!"

THAT NIGHT Cassandra went to sleep quickly. In the other bed across the room, Tanis let her thoughts roam.

After Cassandra's heartrending appeal, Gregg had found soothing words with which to comfort her. Although Tanis had done so much to earn sufficient money for the treatment Cassandra needed, she had doubted, deep down, whether Cassandra would ever be able to walk with the freedom with which she had in the past. Sighing, she put aside her problems and drifted into sleep.

The sisters were having breakfast when Frankie arrived. He ruffled Cassandra's hair—an action that he knew she hated—and gave her a brief kiss on her cheek. She turned her face away and he said in an affected tone, "Oh, we're on our high horse, are we?"

Cassandra continued eating her boiled egg, delving into it with the concentration of a prospector looking for gold. "We're moving away," she told him, "to Dr. Barratt's house. Next Saturday. I won't need you any-

more." She waited for the answer she wanted. It did not come.

Frankie went around to Tanis, but she was ready for the hand ruffling. She ducked, but that was, as she discovered, a wrong move. His hand made contact with her neck and he took immediate advantage of the fact. His fingers moved upward toward her hairline, but she turned, furious with him both for touching her and for doing so in front of her distraught sister.

"Will Tanis need me anymore?" he goaded, grinning.

"Leave me alone," Tanis cried.

"Okay." He made for the door. "From now on the partnership of Anderson and Foster is nonexistent. It'll be Anderson, just Anderson."

"Frankie!" Tanis's cry was frantic. "Come back."

He did come back. "Make up your mind," he said, putting his hand back on Tanis's neck. He cast a sly glance at Cassandra, who was still determinedly eating her egg.

Tanis was caught. There was a pain inside her somewhere and she knew exactly how a rabbit snared by a trap felt. Cassandra threw down her egg spoon and maneuvered her chair toward the door.

"I've lost my appetite," she flung over her shoulder and disappeared down the hall.

Tanis groped for Frankie's wrist, found it and jerked it away. Having counted up to five, she turned, her temper under control. "What do you want?"

"My partner. There's work to do. Two responses so far from that leaflet you put out. A living room in one house, two bedrooms in the other."

"That's great, Frankie. Have you given them quotes for the work?"

He nodded. "And clinched the deals. We start on the bedrooms today. I've got the van outside. It's not far from here, just a few blocks."

"Usual conditions, Frankie? We go halves with the money?"

"Usual conditions," he agreed.

Tanis collected the dishes, stacked them on the draining board and ran along the hall to find Cassandra. She was painting quietly and looked as serene as a girl in love who knew she was loved back. *I didn't realize,* Tanis reflected, *that my sister was so good at acting.*

"Work has come in from those leaflets. Isn't that great?" Tanis told her.

"I heard Frankie tell you. Yes, it's great." She continued attending to her paints and brushes, which were spread on a table next to her. "Don't worry about me. Mrs. Yardley will give me lunch like she did when you were away."

"I'm going to change." Nothing, it seemed, would make Cassandra look at her. Tanis bent down. "Can't you see it's not my fault, Cassie?" she whispered pleadingly.

Cassandra looked at her at last, but her expression was so poignant and so piteous Tanis could hardly bear it.

THEY WERE IN the smaller of the two bedrooms of the house in which they'd been commissioned to work. The initial preparations were behind them. The furniture had been moved by a thoughtful client and now the carpets were covered for protection. Tanis had taken down the curtains—something many people forgot to do, she had discovered.

Together she and Frankie were filling cracks in the plaster and generally making good the entire area that was to be decorated. For a time they worked in silence. Then Tanis said accusingly, "You didn't keep your promise to go and see Cassandra while I was away. Oh, I know you'll say you did, but what's one visit of ten

minutes in nearly forty-eight hours?'' She added, ''She was terribly upset, Frankie.''

''Look—'' he stopped working ''—I'm sorry she had that accident. I'm sorry she's in that chair. She's a nice girl, a lovely girl. But you've got to see it my way. I like moving around. I like dancing and going out. Can't she understand? I like her, but to me now she's just like a kid sister.'' He continued working.

There it was, straight from the hip, Tanis thought, with a lump in her throat for Cassandra. Life just wasn't fair, she decided. Aloud she said, ''All right, but at least you could leave me alone when she's there.''

That, Tanis discovered, had been the wrong thing to say. He came across to her, his hands white with the plaster filler he was applying.

''Leave you alone, darling? I'd have to have a strait-jacket put on me to make me keep my hands to myself when you're around. Or—'' he glanced at his hands ''—this stuff. You're luscious—you must know that. You've had enough guys of your own buzzing around you to know it by now. And don't tell me you've never—''

''No, I've never, ever. Did you get that, Frankie Anderson? And what's more, I'm keeping myself to myself until I find one I can love—really love.''

''Yeah, that's Cassandra's sister talking. She told me that tale, too.''

''When you asked her to live with you? Before her accident, of course.''

''Sarcastic, sweetheart?'' He shook his head. ''It just bounces off me. Of course it was before her accident.''

''She told me. Okay, so she and I are two of a kind. I'm glad. We were brought up by our mother to be fastidious.''

''Why don't you say choosy? Then you'd be speaking my language. I suppose what you mean is, as long as the guy's got a big enough car and bank balance....'' He

ducked as a paintbrush came his way. "Now, now," he warned, "do that once too often and you'll be breaking up a nice little partnership. And if you think I'm going to lay off you just in case I upset your little sister—"

There was a tap at the door and the lady of the house entered with a tray of coffee.

They worked late at the house, making a start on the second bedroom to allow the first to dry out. By the end of the day Tanis was exhausted. Frankie dropped her outside her home and left her, saying he would call for her the next morning.

Even as she opened the front door, she sensed that all was not as it should have been. She pulled off her jacket and hurried into the living room. Cassandra was not there. Feeling concerned now, Tanis went into the kitchen, which was as empty as the living room. It was in the bedroom that she saw the wheelchair. It was as empty as everywhere else, and to Tanis at that moment it was the most frightening sight she had ever seen. Cassandra had gone, but where?

Tanis raced up the stairs, calling her tenant's name. Mrs. Yardley was out. She raced down again, hoping to find at least a note. As she reached the foot of the stairs, the telephone rang. Diving for it, she asked breathlessly, "Yes?"

"I've been trying to contact you from five o'clock onward." It was Gregg at his most unapproachable. Tanis detected a note of reprimand, as well.

"I wasn't having fun, if that's what you think. We worked late on the place we were decorating. Gregg, Cassandra's missing." Her voice had risen. "Something must have happened to her, somebody must have—"

"The 'somebody' was myself. I came, I took her away. Now what are you going to do about it?"

Tanis choked back a gasp. "Took her away? What do you mean? You had no right to come into this house and—and kidnap her."

"I could hardly be accused of kidnapping when I was invited to do everything I did."

"You're lying; you must be. Cassie would never do such a thing without consulting me."

"I have an unpalatable piece of news for you. You aren't her most favorite person at this moment."

"I want to talk to her, Gregg. You see, there was a misunderstanding over Frank Anderson."

There was a moment's silence, a sound of voices muffled by a covering hand. "I'm sorry, but your sister refuses to talk to you." Another pause, then, "Your move."

"No—" Tanis was fighting the hysteria "—your move."

"Maybe I'd better explain. This morning, after you'd gone, Cassandra phoned me here. I was as usual at the hospital in London. My housekeeper promised to try to contact me. I was out of the operating room a little later than I expected—in time for a delayed lunch. I was given Mrs. Casey's message. I contacted her, and she informed me that a young lady called Cassandra Foster had phoned and seemed in a distressed state. Are you still there?"

Tanis whispered, "I'm here."

"I called your number. Cassandra answered. She told me you were deliberately taking Frank Anderson away from her and she couldn't stand seeing you both playing around. She wanted to get out of that house and away from you."

"She's never said such things before."

"There was nowhere before for her to run to, no one to talk to."

"If she felt that way, she should have told me."

There was no response.

"Look, Gregg," Tanis said, "I know you won't understand, nor will she, but Frankie and I are business partners. I rely on him for so many things, like doing

the fancy work, just as he relies on me to do the mundane, uncomplicated painting—''

"Don't stretch your brain to its limits in an effort to explain your relationship with him."

"We don't *have* a relationship," Tanis shouted. "For heaven's sake, Gregg—''

"Be ready for me when I come for you on Saturday," he interrupted curtly and hung up.

On the journey from London to Gregg's house, Tanis did not speak unless Gregg spoke to her. This was infrequent, since the traffic was heavy and driving required all his attention.

Tanis recalled that after telling Mrs. Yardley, her tenant, of her decision to join her sister at Dr. Barratt's home, the older woman had said eagerly, "I hope you don't mind my mentioning it, Miss Foster, but I know another lady, a nurse like me, who'd be very glad to be allowed to rent the downstairs rooms."

Gregg had advised Tanis to let Mrs. Yardley's friend have the apartment for a mutually acceptable period, as soon as an agreement had been signed. Mrs. Yardley had said she was delighted and would pass the message on to her friend.

Now Tanis looked out of the car window at the approach to the village in which Gregg lived. The main street was unusually quiet. Gregg turned the car into the driveway in front of the house and cut the engine. His hand covered Tanis's.

"A word before we go in," he said.

Tanis guessed what was coming. She looked around her, seeing the country beauty, hearing the hiss of the wind through the trees, her ears exquisitely receptive to the birdsong.

"Tell me—'' his glance was cool and held no friendliness "—is it the thought that you couldn't live without Frank Anderson that's kept you so silent since we left?"

Tanis sank back, wishing she could turn her hand and grip his until she inflicted the pain his words were inflicting on her. "Will nothing I say on that subject convince you? Just let me live my own life in my own way."

"Don't you mean mess up your life?" he asked coldly.

Feeling the way I do about you, she thought miserably, *and coming to live where you live, is as good a start as any at messing it up, knowing how badly you regard me. And how out of reach you are, anyway, with a woman of your own who's just waiting for her freedom before you and she....*

"And don't mess up Cassandra's life, either."

The note of warning in his curt words aroused her. "What do you think I am," she demanded, "a vindictive bitch of a girl who blatantly takes away her sister's boyfriend while she sits helplessly looking on?"

He had swiveled sideways so that his elbow rested on the rim of the steering wheel. His attitude of contemplating her as though she were an interesting medical case roused her to a bitter rage.

"Haven't I looked after Cassandra every night and day since her accident?" she stormed. "Haven't I worked long hours to earn money for our keep? Haven't I stood in all weathers at that roadside stand, in markets, at garden fetes, selling Cassandra's paintings to raise money for the treatment she needs to get her back to normal? And you sit there accusing me of messing up Cassandra's life?"

"I'm not criticizing your sisterly love, your loyalty or your devotion. Only your morals."

"My *morals*? You criticize my morals?" Her furious eyes burned into his. "What about yourself? That Lola, that woman I met when I came here for the weekend—the woman you're going to marry? Yet you've kissed me...I've lost count of how many times."

"What's in a kiss?"

His callous dismissal of what had meant so much to her had her swallowing a shriek of anguish. When her self-control had reasserted itself, she found that she was able to accept the truth. That this man would ever regard her as anything but a spiteful man stealer was as unlikely as the moon's taking the place of the sun as the provider of the earth's greatest source of energy.

"YOUR SISTER'S LOOKING FORWARD TO SEEING YOU," Gregg informed her as they entered the house to the warm welcome of the housekeeper.

"Lunch in half an hour, Dr. Barratt?" Mrs. Casey asked.

Gregg nodded, opening the door that gave access to the living room. Cassandra sat in a wheelchair at the window, absorbed in her painting. Distracted by the noise, she looked up. Impatience gave way to wonder, then a spontaneous delight. The light in one pair of brown eyes ignited the light in the other.

"Tanis!" Cassandra put aside her work and held out her arms. The quarrel, it seemed, had been temporarily forgotten. The hug was long and affectionate, and as Tanis looked into her sister's face she said, "It's good to see you looking so well."

Cassandra smiled happily. "Gregg's been wonderful," she exclaimed. "I've had no money, so I haven't been able to give him anything for my keep, but he said it didn't matter."

"I'll remedy that," Tanis assured her quietly, holding Gregg's eyes. "I'm finding work in this area—"

"In your own line," Cassandra said, pulling her work table into position, "you couldn't work alone. You wouldn't get the contracts."

Tanis sat down. "I realize that. That's why I'll be contacting Frankie."

It was as if by saying the name Tanis had pulled an invisible string. Cassandra's head lifted sharply. She

seemed about to speak but did not. It was enough to tell Tanis that her sister's feelings toward Frank Anderson had certainly not changed.

Involuntarily Tanis sought the cool amber eyes that gazed at her from behind Cassandra's chair. The expression in them made her shiver. Clutching her bag, she felt like a patient after a medical examination awaiting the doctor's diagnosis. Except that in this case she knew exactly what that diagnosis was.

CHAPTER SIX

"DID YOU KNOW Gregg has a girl friend?" Cassandra asked conversationally as Tanis saw her into bed that evening.

Tanis's heart leaped, then she told herself she was stupid to be so shocked at the statement. Of course she knew about the woman. But she had never taken seriously the woman's supposed attachment to Gregg. When the woman had come that weekend, he had seemed so unloverlike toward her.

"I did know," Tanis admitted casually.

"Sometimes she comes back here with him from the hospital," Cassandra confided. "She works with him. Did you know that?"

Tanis nodded.

"I don't like her," Cassandra went on, her dark hair spread over the pillow as Tanis tidied away the clothes. "She told me there's not much hope that I'll ever get back to normal again."

Tanis dared not meet her sister's eyes.

When Cassandra spoke again, she seemed shocked. "Do you think she's right? Because if she is—" her face turned into the pillow "—I don't know that I'll want to go on living!"

Sobs shook her small frame and Tanis hurried to her sister's side.

"F-Frankie doesn't like me now, but I've kept telling him, 'When I'm better, when I'm on my feet again....' If I don't get back to normal he'll hate me, hate me!"

"Hush." Tanis held her close. "We're saving up for the very best treatment, aren't we?"

"I can't keep on painting forever. And if the treatment isn't going to do me any good, what's the use of saving?"

"I'll speak to Gregg, Cassie. He'll do something; I know he will."

Tanis wished she could feel as certain as she sounded that Gregg would be able to wave a magic wand and produce a cure, when his own lady friend, a nurse, had effectively dashed all hope.

Gregg was downstairs looking out over the darkening garden, hands in the pockets of the slacks into which he had changed. He did not turn at Tanis's entry.

"Gregg—" she said.

"I heard the conversation. I was in my bedroom opposite yours."

"So you know the question I was going to ask."

"I know it." He did not elaborate as Tanis had hoped he would.

Tanis found a seat, played with the thin gold chain around her neck. "Cassandra's getting desperate, Gregg. Otherwise I wouldn't dream of troubling you. I hate taking advantage of a person's position in life, of his or her contacts, but you're—well, you're a kind of last hope."

He turned and there was no understanding in his expression. "First things first, don't you agree?" His voice grated. "Give her back Frank Anderson."

Tanis sat forward, clutching the chair arms. "I don't *have* Frank Anderson. He's not mine to return."

Gregg swiveled an armchair so that it faced her, sat down and said, "Every time you speak to him, your every reaction when he touches you, even in public, belies that statement."

"That's for—" *Business reasons,* she had been going to say. She sought for other words with which to con-

vince him. But did it really matter? She told herself bitterly that no matter what she might say, Gregg still
would not believe her.

For her own sake, she had to try. Her voice pleaded
for his reasoned judgment of her relationship with
Frankie. "Frank's not in my league," she stated flatly.
"He's an artist and as such accepts few barriers in his
life or in his work. I—I like dividing lines, clearly defined boundaries."

"You do?" The cynical inflection showed how
unconvinced he remained, as did the sarcasm when he
continued, "You like things in their place, tidily, just
where they belong?"

Tanis took the question at its face value and nodded.
This was neutral ground, familiar and safe to tread.
Maybe appealing to his considerable intellect would
bring about an improvement in his attitude toward her.

"Which," she enlarged, "is why I keep to the routine
painting—horizontals, verticals, the woodwork...
straightforward and no straying."

Ignoring the sardonic quirk of his eyebrow, she
pressed on, "Frankie likes a sweep of color, extravagant
mixtures, paper, materials that make an impact." She
sat back in the chair. "I suppose it all fits in with the
flamboyant side of his nature that he seems to have."

Gregg's body was still but his eyes watched her constantly, seeming intrigued by her changing facial expres-
sions, her restrained and stiff movements—which, she
was aware, told him how shy she still was in his
presence.

"How did Cassandra get caught up with Anderson?"

"She met him at a disco. I tried to warn her not to
take him too seriously."

Now his smile taunted as he threw a challenge at her.
"Maybe she thought you were warning her off him
because you wanted him for yourself."

"No!" She sat forward. "Will you stop your insinua-

tions that I'm a liar? He's not what I want in a man. He does nothing for me, nothing!''

"So whenever I see you running after him, you expect me to believe that it's because you can't do without him as a business partner. Come on, Tanis, I'm not one of your naive young friends.''

Exasperated by his intransigent attitude, she cried, "How many times do I have to tell you black is black before you stop calling it white?''

Having created havoc with her emotions and seeming satisfied with his achievement, Gregg resumed his relaxed position. His hooded glance took in the hugging fit of her high-buttoned dress, the way it followed the fullness of her shape.

The half-lowered lids hinted tantalizingly at the man beneath the impassive exterior of the doctor. Tanis's pulse rate increased as she remembered how many times she had been in his arms.

"What's a kiss?'' he had said carelessly, but hadn't there been more to what had happened between them than a mere meeting of the lips? And once, she recalled, she had as good as let him know that he had the power to hurt her, had almost let him know how much she cared. Once, also, he had told her how much pleasure she would give a man if she let him make love to her. *A man,* she reflected, *any man, not just this one....*

"Shall we change the subject and talk about Cassandra?'' he suggested. "That's what you intended to do when you left her in bed, wasn't it? I heard you tell her.''

"I started to talk about it,'' she commented tartly. "It was you who introduced the irrelevant subject of Frank Anderson.''

"Hardly irrelevant—'' he leaned forward in the chair, hands clasped loosely "—since it concerned her emotional well-being. In other words, resolving that problem would be of considerable help in making her

determined to recover, thus ensuring that any treatment she might receive would have a greater chance of success."

Tanis held his gaze steadfastly, nodding firmly in agreement.

"Which would mean breaking any emotional connection you may have with Frank Anderson."

Despite the provoking words, her gaze did not falter.

He seemed irritated by her silence. "Are you with me?" he asked.

"All the way." Her heart added, *until my dying day.*

For a moment he was silent, then he said, his manner entirely professional, "I'm sure you realize she requires more surgery." Tanis nodded, her only sign of tension being in her clenched hands. "As I explained when we first met, orthopedics is not my line. However, I have a friend and colleague who specializes in orthopedic surgery at the hospital at which I'm also a surgeon."

Tanis's hands ached, her breathing was shallow, her whole body waiting, hoping. . . .

"My sweet Tanis—" his voice was softly caressing, yet still edged with authority "—if you don't relax here and now, I shall soon have to treat you for shock."

His gentle reprimand achieved its objective and she laughed, the tension leaving her; but even so she could not entirely relax. The tip of her tongue ran over her dry lips, and with a shaking hand she pushed back her hair. Gregg watched her, concerned yet clinical. He was all doctor now.

"We've been saving, Gregg," Tanis said at last. "It wouldn't be enough to pay for the complete treatment, but there's quite a bit now, and if Cassandra paints some more and I find work—"

His curt nod checked her, but the enthusiasm did not leave her. She hung on his every word.

"Cassandra would need to be examined," he continued. "The medical notes from her past treatment

would be required. Her own doctor would have to be informed."

"But he's in London. Now that we're living here she would be changing doctors anyway, wouldn't she?"

He nodded. "That takes time. The surgeon's name is Russell Mansfield."

"He's good, Gregg?"

"One of the best in his field, Tanis."

He smiled and her heart spun like a top. She wanted to run to him, fling her arms around his neck and thank him...and let all her love for him come tumbling from her lips.

Looking away for fear of his guessing her secret, she said, "There's still the question of the fee."

"Will you leave it alone?"

She took a breath to protest, saw the rebuke and let out her breath in a sigh. "You're being so good to us, I just don't know how to express my gratitude. I'll never be able to pay you back—"

"Oh, but you will." His voice was deceptively soft. He rose, holding out his hand. "Stand up, Tanis." There was no disobeying an order given in that tone. She stood uncertainly, shyly questioning.

"Now," he commanded, "kiss me." At her shocked expression he added, "Kiss me as you would your lover."

If this was Gregg's way of letting her thank him, then she would with all her heart. She smiled, lifted her arms—but found she couldn't even touch him. There was inside her a driving force that made her long to do so, but it was no use; she just couldn't overcome her shyness.

"Those dividing lines?" he queried softly. "Those clearly defined boundaries inhibiting you?"

She nodded, glad that he understood. When he spoke again, it was to prove that, understand though he might, he was dismissing the reason out of hand.

"You'll have to cross those boundaries for once. You're not going to your bed tonight until you do. Maybe to mine, but not to yours. Have you got that?" There was no tenderness in his eyes to encourage her.

Angrily she lifted her arms again, this time locking them around his neck. The anger made her reckless. She'd kiss him, she thought; she'd show him he didn't frighten her with his threats.

Her arms crossed behind his neck, but his head did not move under her pressure. She found herself having to impel it down, standing on tiptoe to reach his mouth. He still did not help her, letting his arms stay at his sides.

Oh, she would kiss him, take that sarcastic smile from his face; she would— When their lips made contact, hers pressing against his, it was like a toboggan ride of sensation swishing inside her head. Her feelings joined in the joyous descent, leaving a sparkling trail in the brightness of her eyes. He had bent a little, just enough to make it easier for her to exert even greater pressure. But still he did not kiss her back.

Her ears picked up small pleading sounds, like a pet wanting to be noticed. When she realized the noises were coming from her own throat, she was beyond caring. She had to make this man respond, to acknowledge her as a desirable woman, to lift his arms and hold her to him. In her desperation she held away, probing his eyes and finding them laughing at her.

Again her mouth came at his. Her hands moved to find his hair, to run over his stubble-roughened cheeks. At last her lips parted and her tongue ventured through to get the taste of him, to take it into her and....

His arms came around her, and when he crushed her against him there were no barriers left for him to overcome. She herself had thrown them aside in her efforts to make him respond. Her whole body burned with

desire, with the need to be held by him, to be lost in him, to be loved by him.

She had been in his arms before, had received his kisses, his caresses, but it had never been like this. Then she had been the prey. Now she had played the predator and she was shaken to her depths by the experience. Of its own accord her body urged against the hardness of his, feeling the muscles move beneath the surface of his body, the punishing angles of his hips and knees against her, his ribs and chest compressing her breasts.

At last he eased her away, but a hand had found its way to the swelling curve of a breast. His lips trailed her warm cheeks and he said against her throat, "You want my help in arranging treatment for your sister?"

Tanis nodded against his chest, feeling the dark hairs through the silk of his shirt. His caressing fingers over her breast were arousing her unbearably.

"I'll help you on one condition," he told her. Now her body stiffened in his arms. "That you let the world know you're my woman."

"That's blackmail! I've never been any man's woman!" Tanis had pulled away and was straightening her dress.

He smoothed back his hair and slipped his hands into his pockets. His breadth of shoulder, his authoritative bearing, the firm if slightly curving lips, made him intimidating yet magnetic, unreachable yet possessing a drawing power that maddened with its strength. "Nevertheless, it's one of those barriers that you'll have to overcome—if you want my assistance in arranging Cassandra's treatment."

"It's unethical," she hit back. "I never thought a man who's reached the heights of his profession as you've done would stoop to such tactics."

"And what about your tactics in taking your sister's boyfriend from her while she sits helplessly looking on?"

"Just now you implied I was an innocent. So how could I have taken Frank Anderson away?"

"Maybe he's been a bit slower in breaking down your barriers than I've been?"

Her hand lifted, but she let it fall. How could she hit out physically at a man who had been so good to her and Cassandra? He had watched the action with amusement and she knew that if she had followed her initial intention through to its conclusion, his hand would have replied in kind.

Tanis made to sit down, but he caught her arms and pulled her back to face him. "I want an answer."

Their bodies were touching again and she gazed up into his eyes, which were seeking her answer. She found desire gazing back at her, plus an undoubted appetite of a purely sexual nature, and there was certainly mockery. "No love," she murmured, her hand lifting to touch his partly buttoned shirt. "You want me to be your woman without love?"

"Give me one good reason for loving you."

Her cheek turned to rest against his shoulder, an action arising from the new familiarity between them. Sighing, she replied, "I can't think of any."

His hands stayed in his pockets. If she reached up to kiss him again, would that bring his arms around her? Or was he really as unmoved by her nearness as he appeared? The idea stirred her to anger again.

Breaking away, she asked, "How would you refer to me among your friends and colleagues? Fiancée? Wife-to-be?"

"As my woman."

"But that's degrading. I'll be nobody's woman."

"Not even for your sister's sake?" There was derision in his smile; pleasure, too, at having trapped her.

"You're unspeakable," she retorted. Her eyes ran over him, hoping to convey contempt, but revealing instead her admiration, her wish to mean something to

him, to be looked upon by the world in which they moved as the woman he was going to marry.

"I can see from your face that you're battling against those rigid lines you've drawn around yourself. If you want that help, I'm warning you, you'll have to erase them forever."

She walked to the window, lifting the curtain on the darkened gardens. Break through her natural reticence, her reserve, uncaring if friends and acquaintances— Gregg's acquaintances, too—smiled on her just a little differently because she wore no ring, carried no label except that of Gregg's woman?

"Your lady friend and colleague wouldn't like it," she suggested, hoping that by jolting his conscience about Lola she could make him back down from his demand.

"Lola is irrelevant to this situation," he dismissed the suggestion sharply. "At present, until her divorce comes through, she remains married—to someone else."

Turning, Tanis said, "In that case, why—if I agree to your suggestion—couldn't you call me your fiancée?" He stayed unresponsive and she could not keep the hurt from her eyes. "I can see," she flung at him, "you haven't any finer feelings, no understanding of how I might feel when—when people look at me, then at you, and wonder...."

Throwing him a pained, exasperated look, she turned back to the darkness outside. Through the reflection on the windowpane she saw him approaching, felt his hands lower softly to her shoulders, then move to hold her breasts. A lightning bolt of feeling shot through her body and she had to fight the impulse to turn and be enfolded in his arms.

"What's really worrying you, Tanis? The fact that you'd lose Frank Anderson out of your life?"

She stirred restlessly under his caressing thumbs. "I might already have lost him." Too late she realized that

he might regard her words as signifying that he must have been in her life in order to have "lost" him.

That her guess had been correct revealed itself in the way he pushed her from him and returned to the center of the room. Afraid that by her prevarication and her unguarded statement she had made him retract his offer, she turned and ran to him.

"I'll be your woman, Gregg," she promised fervently. "If it means losing my—my self-respect, then at least I'd be losing it for a good cause. Nothing you demand of me will make me stand in the way of Cassandra's return to full health."

A smile tightened on his lips and he asked, eyeing her broodingly, "Nothing? Not even if I insist on your carrying through the charade and becoming my woman in private?"

She frowned, uncertain again. "You didn't say that was included in the deal."

"I didn't say it wasn't."

Her palms covered her cheeks. "You're asking a great deal of me. I like you, I—I respect you, I—" Just in time she cut off the word "love." Her eyes sought his. "I want you to—to respect me. But you won't, you won't if I—if I. . . ." She swung away. "I can't do it, Gregg."

Hands turned her, cupped her face, tilted it back. His mouth touched hers, lightly, teasingly, his lips playing with and finally parting hers. Having gained the access he wanted, he took her into his arms. If her willingness to go into them, her eager acceptance of his searching kisses, her almost frenzied return of them, told him much more than she wanted him to know, she did not care. *I'll be your woman,* she wanted to cry, *in public, in private, in heaven itself. . .*

TANIS AWOKE alert and energetic after a good night's sleep. The sky was cloudy, but to her eyes the day was bright. Gregg had not objected when she had told him she wanted to work, thus adding to the money she was saving for Cassandra's treatment. It would also pay for their keep while they lived in his house.

It was Monday morning and she had to catch him before he went off to London. Pulling on a jacket over her silky pajamas, she hurried out of the bedroom. His door was open and she dashed across, certain she would find the room empty. He was pulling on his shirt. When he saw her, he stopped.

Surprise colored his eyes, then they narrowed. "Come to kiss your man good morning?"

Flustered by his words and the sight of his hair-darkened chest, by the flat stomach below which his well-fitting trousers rested on hard hipbones, she stammered, "Y-yes...no! I wanted to catch you before you went out to ask you whether...." He was not listening. He was walking toward her, his crooked smile showing that his thoughts were on things other than everyday matters. They were, in fact, on the slim figure beneath the clinging pajamas.

His shirt hung open and when his arms closed around her, pulling her against him, her cheek had no place to rest except against his chest. With impatience his hands found their way beneath her pajama top to hold her bare waist, then slide up to rest on her ribs.

Wonderingly she looked at him, and his mouth touched down on her upraised lips. She was sure that his practiced hands could feel the throb of her body as it responded madly to the touch of him. Slowly his hands moved again, and with a soundless gasp at the feel of his palms holding possessively the roundness of her breasts, she pressed her cheek against him again.

It was part shyness, part longing to show him how she reveled in his proprietary attitude toward her. His

caresses lighted a flame inside her that threatened to grow into a miniature inferno. She whispered, "Please, Gregg, don't. Not now, *please*."

"Which implies I can continue later?" He examined her flushed face and overly bright eyes. "You look as radiant as if we'd spent the night together."

"I—I'm a good actress, aren't I?" she responded. "Playing the part of your woman, I mean."

"Acting be damned," he muttered. "I'd call this the real thing—if I didn't know it wasn't."

Tanis twisted and turned and freed herself. Wrapping her jacket lightly around her, she said, "I came to speak to you, not to give you the opportunity to make love to me."

A quick look at his watch had him saying, "If I had the time I'd prove you wrong. But you've delayed me long enough. And—" he stopped her protest before she had begun "—don't tell me it wasn't your fault. You shouldn't have invited yourself into my bedroom. What do you want?"

"You remember you agreed I could continue with my work?" He nodded, fastening his shirt buttons. "And you remember that when—" she was on less firm ground here "—when I came to stay that weekend you agreed that if I came to live here, you'd give me and—and Frank Anderson the job of redecorating your house?"

"Did I?" His eyes were cool and it was as if she had never felt the electrifying touch of his hands on her body. She had known that the mere mention of Frankie's name would affect him, but she had not imagined how cold she would feel when the suspicion and distrust took the warmth from his eyes.

"Yes, you did," she persisted, "and I'm sure you do remember. I was hoping to get your permission to contact Frank today, so he could come and look around. Then we could give you an estimate—"

He pulled on his jacket. "Do as you wish," he said coldly and pushed past her, making for the stairs.

Tanis phoned Frankie and caught him just before he left for work.

"I was wondering," he said, "when I'd hear from you. Where does Foster and Anderson stand now that you've moved house?"

"It still exists," Tanis answered quickly. "What's more, I've got work for us—that is, if Dr. Barratt accepts our estimate for the work that needs doing here."

"You mean the great man himself has agreed to let me show my face in his house? What's more, work there?" Tanis did not answer. "Well, when can I come?"

It would be better, Tanis thought, if Gregg were not around when Frankie came. "Hold on," she said. "I'll speak to Mrs. Casey."

The housekeeper was busy in the kitchen. "Dr. Barratt won't be home for a few days, Miss Foster," she informed Tanis. "He told me this morning that after his sessions at the hospital he'll be staying at his apartment in London."

Returning to the phone, she said, "What about this evening, Frankie?"

"Okay with me. Will the doctor be in attendance?" He had upgraded his accent in an attempt at mimicking.

"If you mean Gregg, he's away for the moment. Frankie, there's something I'd like to ask."

"You mean don't upmarket the price like I've just upmarketed my vocal chords?"

"Nothing like that. It's Cassandra, Frankie." Tanis had lowered her voice. "*Please* will you be nice to her? Make her think she's special, fuss over her a bit? She—she still likes you a lot, Frankie." There was a heavy silence from the other end. "Gregg knows someone—a specialist in orthopedics—who might be able to work a near miracle and get her on her feet again."

"You mean as she used to be?" Frankie's tone was cautious.

In contrast, Tanis's answer was incautious. "Yes, yes, back to normal, so she can walk again, just like the old days."

"And dance again? Go out to parties, join in everything?"

"Yes, Frankie, yes." Tanis knew she was doing wrong in speaking so optimistically of Cassandra's future mobility, but she convinced herself it was right if it brought Frankie back to her sister. Anyway, Tanis consoled her conscience, maybe this man was so clever he *could* work near miracles. And now that she'd agreed to Gregg's condition, she hoped he would waste no time in contacting the surgeon and that events would move quickly.

There was a sigh in her ear. "Okay, I'll be good to your little sister. I'll kiss her and hold her hand and—"

"Take her for walks in her chair?"

Tanis could almost feel Frankie wince. "Okay—that, too. Anything to get that decorating contract."

Tanis wished his words had been kinder, but at least he had agreed to her request. "Eight o'clock?" she suggested. "We'll have finished dinner by then."

" 'Dinner,' is it? We're moving in some high-and-mighty circles now, aren't we?" Tanis did not answer. "Eight tonight," Frankie added. "See you." He hung up.

"Tanis?" Cassandra's voice came distantly from her bedroom and Tanis raced upstairs to tell her sister the news.

FRANKIE ARRIVED EARLY. The housekeeper looked with interest at the visitor. He had tidied his manners as well as his appearance and he smiled at Mrs. Casey with disarming sincerity. It was, Tanis knew, the "other" Frank Anderson, the young man with artistic ability and

insight that lurked beneath the layabout image he liked to project.

Cassandra had been delighted when he bent down to kiss her and she reached up to hold him. He made no movement of objection and Tanis thought he was merely keeping his promise to be nice to her sister—until he lifted his head and she saw genuine warmth in his face.

As he examined the house, he took measurements with which Tanis helped him. He discussed the type of paint and paper or other materials he considered would be advisable on the many different surfaces that would have to be covered.

Back in the main sitting room, where Cassandra sat painting while glowing with pride at Frankie's professionalism, Frank filled the back of a large envelope with figures and sums in his effort to arrive at an estimate of the cost of the work. On another piece of paper he wrote the total sum and tossed it to Tanis.

"Give that to your good friend the doctor and tell him it's not final."

"I know that," Tanis responded irritably. "How can it be when we don't know exactly what he wants?"

"Show me," Cassandra demanded. "Well, to me that's a lot of money, but to Gregg, I think maybe he'll think you're doing it at a discount!"

"Okay—" Frankie pretended to seize the piece of paper "—let's add a couple of zeros to that estimate."

"That," Tanis objected, "would be unscrupulous. And that's one thing I know you're not, Frankie."

"Oh, no?" Frankie queried glibly, moving toward Tanis, arm extended with the aim of encompassing her waist.

Guessing his intention, and knowing Cassandra's eyes were on them, she slipped sideways to stand beside the wheelchair. "He's not unscrupulous, is he, Cassandra?" she asked, to gloss over the incident.

"He's lots of things," Cassandra answered, smiling gaily, "but not that."

Tanis gave a silent sigh of relief, watching as Frankie responded to her sister's provocation. Leaving them together, she went up to her bedroom, returning downstairs only when Frankie shouted that he was going.

"Tell me when the lord of the manor is back in residence," he said, grinning cheekily. "That maybe he'll give me an audience and we'll go around the place together and work out in detail what he's got in mind. Be nice to him and give him everything he wants, as I know only you know how—"

"What are you talking about?" Cassandra called indignantly from her chair. "What does Tanis give Gregg?"

"You'd be surprised," Frank answered spitefully. "I've caught them in so many different—"

"Stop it!" Tanis said hoarsely.

"—that if I wanted to blackmail his Lordship," Frankie went smoothly on, "I could do it just like that." He snapped his fingers.

"And lose the decorating contract," Tanis returned fiercely.

"So I keep my mouth shut," he answered, then left the house.

"Now tell me what all that was about," Cassandra ordered, putting aside her work.

Tanis shrugged, then decided to tell her sister the partial truth. "Gregg and I,—well—we've got an understanding." As Cassandra's eyes grew wider, Tanis added quickly, "It's not what you think it is, Cassie. Well, not quite." What she herself did not know was how closely Gregg would adhere to his statement that they would let the world know she was his "woman."

"But Tanis, that's great, just—"

"Cassie, please—just let it be, will you?"

Cassandra looked a little hurt but commented, "If

that's what you want." She looked up. "Tanis, it means...." Relief was like the sun breaking through. "It means there's nothing between you and Frankie after all?"

Tanis nodded. "There never has been, Cassie, not on my side, nor on Frankie's."

The smile on Cassandra's face grew brighter. "But," she persisted, "there is between you and Gregg?"

"I don't know, Cassandra, I just don't know."

CHAPTER SEVEN

GREGG WAS AWAY four days. To Tanis the hours had dragged. Having nothing else to do, she walked around the entire house again, examining each room to determine how much preparation it would need before the constructive work could begin.

Having done that, she toured the extensive gardens, gazing at the area that would one day be converted into a swimming pool, then standing beside the lily pond and watching the spraying fountain. She went for walks both with and without Cassandra, along the nearby country lanes.

"You must ask Dr. Barratt to take you to Ashdown Forest one weekend," Mrs. Casey told her one morning over breakfast. "It's a beautiful place and has such a history attached to it. There are deer there, fallow deer, aren't there, George?"

George, who had finished his breakfast and was getting ready to go outside to work, nodded. "And badgers," he added, "about four hundred of 'em. Not to mention barn owls and squirrels and foxes."

"Do you know," his wife added, as George went outside, "that on a clear day it's even possible to see the Post Office Tower in London? So you see what an unusual place the forest is." She added doubtfully, "It might be a bit difficult pushing Miss Cassandra through it. In some places it's rough underfoot and there's open heathland."

"That's all right," Cassandra assured her "while they're gone I'll do my painting. I'll be able to see it

when I'm back on my feet—one day I will be, you know."

Mrs. Casey nodded in firm agreement, although Tanis knew that the housekeeper was aware, like everyone else, that a question mark still hung over that possibility.

On Thursday evening Gregg telephoned. Mrs. Casey called out to Tanis. "Dr. Barratt's wanting to talk to you, Miss Foster."

Tanis picked up the receiver. "Tanis here," she said. She did not add, as she longed to do, *it's good to hear your voice.*

"I'm returning home tomorrow evening," Gregg told her. "I'll be bringing Russell Mansfield to dinner. It will give him a chance to meet Cassandra and assess her personally."

"That's wonderful, Gregg. Shall I tell Cassandra?"

"Why not, since she'll be the main reason for his visit. Would you ask Mrs. Casey to provide dinner for four tomorrow evening?"

It was a command and it was the doctor talking. Tanis saw no reason to argue. In fact, she wanted to express her gratitude but recalled Gregg's reaction—the demand of a reward—the last time she had thanked him. Instead she told him, "Frankie's been here."

"Why?"

"I did ask your permission. Before we—Foster and Anderson, I mean—can submit an estimate for the work to be done here, Frankie needed to go over the house, take measurements...." Tanis wished Gregg would make some remark. "He's made a rough estimate but he can't finalize it until you're back and can tell us exactly what you want."

A pause, then, "Which means he'll be wishing his presence on us this weekend?"

Tanis resented the phrasing but answered evenly, "He'll come when he's invited by you."

"Which is never if it means creating havoc in Cassandra's life."

"No, Gregg," Tanis reasoned anxiously. "Before he came I asked him to be especially nice to her, and he was. It was almost as if he had real feelings for her."

"It's surprising what a man will do when there's a job and good money involved."

"Please don't be sarcastic. You'll see what I mean when they're together again."

"I agree. I'll see the actor as well as the artist in him."

By the time Tanis had thought of a retort he had gone.

Tanis chose her dress with care the following evening. It was boldly floral and sleeveless and buttoned to the waist, with the skirt swinging in double pleats to the hem.

Cassandra then demanded her attention. Tanis helped her into a blue-and-white-patterned skirt, with elastized waist and a jacket top to match. Tanis watched as her sister applied makeup, and tried to restrain her from using too much. Cassandra would not listen.

"I want to make myself look older. I want to be admired, Tanis. There's nothing else for a man to look at except my face, you know that."

"Ah," Tanis warned, putting an arm across her shoulder, "self-pity's a banned subject. Never a word of complaint, you promised, after your last operation on your legs, because at least you could get around with crutches."

Cassandra shrugged thin shoulders. "Maybe, but you don't know what goes on in my mind."

From behind Cassandra's chair Tanis put her arms around her sister's neck. "Two things, Cassie. One, Dr. Mansfield might be married, and two, he's sure to be interested in you—in your legs, and then only in a clinical way."

Cassandra pretended to pout. "You do make a girl feel good and attractive."

Tanis smiled and moved away. She herself was filled with a tremendous feeling of happiness. Gregg was coming home.

Cassandra commented, flicking her dark curls, "Anyway, I bet this man Russell is ancient. At least fifty and bald. Or gray—"

"Or both," added Tanis, at which both girls laughed.

"I'm glad," Cassandra remarked, "that Gregg's not bringing that Lola Buxton. She told me she's going to marry him."

Tanis was still, scarcely breathing. "Oh, but didn't you know?" she managed at last. "The woman's still married. Her divorce isn't through yet."

"So she's counting her chickens?" Cassandra asked brightly.

"You mean her Greggs," Tanis replied, and they laughed again.

Russell Mansfield was neither gray nor bald. He was, Tanis estimated having welcomed him and been on the receiving end of his blue-eyed glance, around Gregg's age. What he did not possess, in her eyes, was Gregg's magnetism and intense masculinity.

Whereas Gregg's eyes were veiled and unreadable, Russell Mansfield's were as uncomplicated and easily read as a five-year-old's reading book. His hair was fair and neatly combed, his suit well cut, his manner sincere. He moved restrainedly and possessed an unsophisticated air that to Tanis's sensitive eyes marked him out as a bachelor.

When he turned to greet Cassandra, his hand was checked in its path toward her as if he were a man about to seize a painted ornament, only to discover just in time that it originated in the Ming dynasty.

To Tanis's surprise, there was a sudden color in his cheeks. Cassandra, seeing it and sensing his shyness,

reached out her hand and took his. "Tanis and I," she remarked with a touch of impudence, "thought you might be bald and white haired! Thank goodness you're young and handsome, even though you are a specialist!"

Tanis looked quickly at Gregg, fearing his annoyance, but he was smiling broadly as Cassandra's spontaneous remark made his colleague laugh. The tension that had been present dispersed completely.

For a moment, with the laughter lingering, Tanis's gaze met Gregg's. Her delight at his presence had put a brilliance into her eyes. His eyes glittered back and his hand came out. "Tanis?" It was an invitation, but it was also a command. *Show yourself to be my woman.* She could almost hear him thinking the words. *I'm keeping my side of the bargain. Keep yours.*

Her hesitation was of a moment's duration, but by his tautened mouth she knew that he had noticed. As she went to stand beside him, his arm pulled her close to his side. The others looked surprised, then uncertain. When at last Cassandra smiled, Tanis knew she had just recalled that "understanding" with Gregg. Russell Mansfield, however, looked puzzled.

"Are congratulations called for?" he inquired of Gregg. "I thought you were already involved with another—" He looked swiftly from one to the other. "Forget that, will you? I have a bad habit—" he smiled ruefully "—of putting my two big feet into it."

Tanis knew he was referring to Lola Buxton, who must have been known to him, too, through working at the same hospital. Russell Mansfield's comment had Tanis attempting to break away from Gregg's hold.

"Nothing to put your foot into, Russell," Gregg said, eyeing Tanis lazily. "A man can have a woman—"

Tanis's teeth snapped together. "Will you be quiet?" she urged, realizing at once that she had only made matters worse.

Russell looked uncomfortable and turned an embarrassed smile to Cassandra, who unknowingly eased the tension by putting a finger to her lips.

"Shsh!" she whispered. Again the visitor laughed, and it was as though they, too, shared a secret.

"Missed me, woman?" Gregg's whispered question made her ear tingle exquisitely and did her nervous system no good at all.

In the background she could hear Cassandra and Russell talking, which gave her the courage to snap back untruthfully, "No, I did not!"

"I'll deal with you later." Gregg made the threat quietly, but his eyes drooped to skim the slim shape of her as if he were savoring in advance the pleasures to come.

It seemed that Russell Mansfield was questioning Cassandra about her accident and the treatment that had followed. It had, she told him, been spread over a period of many months. Each time a little progress had been made, but the normal use of her legs had still not been regained.

"That's why we're both saving so hard," Tanis told him, forgetting for the moment that Gregg's arm was still around her. "Cassandra paints and I sell her pictures. We put aside a portion of my earnings—which, unfortunately, fluctuate with customers' demands—to add to the amount."

"If," Cassandra took her up, "if you, Dr. Mansfield, would—would agree to give me treatment, to get me back to walking without crutches, we'd—we'd give you *all* our money and more, as much as you want. Tanis and I will save and save; I'll keep painting, she'll keep selling...."

Russell Mansfield's fair skin was tinged with color. His eyes crinkled in laughter as he turned to Gregg. "You must have done a poor publicity job on me to make these two very pleasant sisters believe I'm so avaricious."

To Cassandra he said, "Miss Foster, I wouldn't touch your money. You would be treated in hospital, by me, like everyone else."

"Dr. Barratt—" Mrs. Casey opened the door "—dinner is about to be served."

The meal was more formal than usual. Instead of taking her usual place at the side of the long dining table, Tanis hesitated, looking from one chair to the other.

"At the end, Miss Foster," Mrs. Casey indicated discreetly.

Tanis frowned. "Are you sure?" Gregg at the head of the table, herself at the foot, as if she were his fiancée, his official hostess?

His faintly derisive glance revealed that he had followed the path of her thoughts. "Tanis, my love— Mrs. Casey is giving you my instructions."

Russell's puzzled frown increased her annoyance at Gregg's openly possessive attitude. What game was he playing? Or was he keeping his word about telling the world that she was his "woman"?

"THANK YOU, GREGG," Cassandra said next morning, "for bringing Dr. Mansfield to see me."

"I'm glad you liked him."

"I don't just like him, I trust him. I'm sure he'll work the miracle I've been waiting for."

Gregg frowned. "I never said he'd do that, Cassandra. Miracles are hard to come by these days, medically as in everything else."

"Oh, but—" her gaze was steady "—I know, I just *know* he'll help me to walk and dance again. Then Frankie will love me as he used to. Tanis—" she twisted in her chair "—Frankie's so patient with me suddenly. He kisses me and talks about the future as if we're going to share it. So you see, Gregg, just the interest Dr. Mansfield's taking in me has worked a miracle there."

Gregg glanced quickly at Tanis, appeared to speak

but remained silent. What had he been going to say, Tanis wondered. And what had that strange look meant? "It—it's a lovely morning," she commented, glancing through the window and hoping to break the strained silence. "Gregg—" she swung to him "—Mrs. Casey said you should take me to Ashdown Forest. Her husband told me about the lovely views from there."

He moved to put his arm across her shoulders. "Is that an order or a request?"

Tanis smiled, making a moue. "An order." At his mock severity she added, "Please?"

"Yes, yes, go today," Cassandra urged. "I'll be fine."

Still holding Tanis, Gregg glanced outside. "Picnic weather." He slid his hand upward and held her by the neck, moving her to the doorway. "Mrs. Casey," he called, "could you put a few sandwiches together?"

The housekeeper appeared at the kitchen door. "For you and Miss Tanis? Are you taking her to the forest, Dr. Barratt? I told her to ask you."

"Ask me, Mrs. Casey? She ordered me." The woman laughed and withdrew.

The roads leading to Ashdown Forest, and cutting through it in places, were quiet. It was early and the visitors and tourists had not yet begun to arrive. Gregg drove slowly so that Tanis could see the varied scenery encompassed by the forest boundary.

There were stretches of heathland rising to the clear sky and crested by trees. Some areas were wild and barren, with perhaps one tree lifting out of scrub and heather. There were hills and valleys, gorse giving a sunlike touch of yellow to the extensive and intense greenery of trees and bushes.

Gregg took the car into a rutted parking area, which itself afforded a view of sweeping landscapes. One line of tree-covered hills after another took the breath away.

Gregg pointed, moving his arm sweepingly. "The

Surrey Mills, across the Medway Valley.'' His finger indicated the skyline. "There you can see from Leith Hill in the North Downs to Wrotham in Kent. And there to the south are the South Downs. Did you know—'' he took Tanis's hand and they walked among the trees ''—that Ashdown Forest is part of the forest of Anderida, which covered Sussex in Roman times? It stretched for one hundred and twenty miles right across southeastern England.''

''And this—'' Tanis looked down with something near to reverence ''—where we're walking, is the same ground as they walked on?''

"Yes and no,'' Gregg answered, amused, "because with the passing of centuries, layers of earth build up and cover the past. But in a sense it's the same, I suppose. The trees are far fewer, of course. Many of the great oaks were felled for the furnaces of the Sussex iron industry. It reached its peak in the sixteenth century at the time of the Spanish Armada. Cannons were made here that apparently found their way to both sides. But even the Romans found a large number of iron workings and they carried it on.''

For a time they walked in silence, as Tanis thought about the past, felt it almost in the great stillness that extended around them. There were the varied songs of birds, trees rustling, whispering of the past.

''If we're lucky we might just see a fallow deer. There are horse trails, too.'' Gregg pointed to hoof marks that had been imprinted into the hard, dry earth. Tanis glanced at him and he netted her eyes in a smile. A flame of warmth like a newly struck match started up inside her. His arm slid around her waist, pulling her close.

As they walked their thighs made fleeting contact and Tanis felt the flame grow, creating a longing for even greater contact. Did Gregg know what he was doing to her, or was it accident that it was now their hips that were pressed one to the other? Under a young

and sturdy pine tree he stopped and pulled her around.

In a moment she was pressed to him, and the brushing of his lips against hers fanned the flame once more as instinctively she sought to capture and hold his wandering kiss.

"Well, woman of mine—" his arms crossed across her back, holding her prisoner "—tell me the truth. Did you miss me? Or did you take over your sister's boyfriend when he had finished playing the lover to her?"

"Isn't the word 'trust' in your vocabulary?" she flared, her brown eyes stormy. "Haven't you got any faith in my integrity? Am I so terrible that even though I'm your 'woman'—you called me that—you still think I'd go not only behind Cassie's back but behind yours, too, and carry on a relationship with another man?"

He was unmoved by her rage and smiled down at her, his eyes cool. "There's no knowing what a woman will do these days. They don't seem to be made of the same stuff as they used to be. God knows, I see enough evidence of that in my daily work at the hospital clinic and in the operating room."

He was not baiting her, she knew that, but she was angry all the same. "What makes me furious," she hit back, her voice low, "is the way you seem to be blind to the fact that my convictions and principles simply wouldn't allow my morals to be knocked off course or swayed just to make them in tune with the times we live in."

"In other words—" they were standing apart as he spoke "—you're saying you have those rare qualities of honesty, straightforwardness and unswerving loyalty."

"Yes," she answered positively.

"I'm glad to hear it." He relaxed and took her hand again. All the same, she wondered if his smile held a twist of cynicism.

He had taken her jacket and the bag that contained the food and flasks. Their footsteps crunched on

heather and bracken. Sometimes the path disappeared, but Gregg assured her that it didn't matter since he knew the forest so well.

"It is possible to get lost in this forest and to forget where you parked your car. You find yourself wanting to wander on—and on again. There's a Roman road through it and medieval trackways."

Tanis nodded. "You'll probably laugh," she remarked, "but I can feel the past. It's here, isn't it, still all round us."

"The place certainly has a long history. It's said that in the fourteenth century the forest was so dense that sixteen or so guides were needed to take travelers from end to end."

"All this—" Tanis gazed around "—only about thirty miles from London. And, Mr. Casey said, within sight of a landmark in the center of London!"

"The Post Office Tower: technology such as was never even dreamed of by Stone Age man when he lived—or so they believe—on the high downs!"

They made their way deep into the forest. When they climbed some of the open tracts of land to gain a seemingly limitless view of the far landscape, Gregg's arm was around her waist.

"It's time we had our food," Gregg said at last. He led her down a slope. "In this hollow. These places catch the sun."

Spreading a weatherproof sheet on the ground, Gregg pulled Tanis down beside him. He peeled off his jacket and placed it beside hers. As he rolled up his shirt sleeves, Tanis saw the strength of his arms, the dark hairs springing, the gold of his watch gleaming as the sun's rays touched it.

He unpacked the food to find that there were sandwiches with varied fillings, jellies in small containers, fruit juice and coffee to drink. They ate in silence, listening to the forest sounds. Now and then Tanis's

glance wandered to the half-reclining figure of her companion. The slacks he wore showed signs of age and were creased across the hips and thighs.

A sensation began deep inside her of longing to match her femininity with the powerful magnetism of his maleness. As her eyes crept upward she found that he had unbuttoned his shirt down to the belt around his lean waist. The dark spread of hair across his chest created in her a desire to touch him, to press her cheeks against his flesh. It grew so strong, she bent her head as if to ward off a faint.

"What's the sum total of your analysis of my sensuality? Do I rate average on the score of qualities you consider necessary for a man to possess?"

"Average, Dr. Barratt?" she answered playfully, to hide the embarrassment she felt at his having been conscious of her regard. "You go right over the top!"

"Which means—" he continued to put away the remains of their picnic "—you have no regrets about that condition I made when I agreed to look for the best medical help available for Cassandra's trouble?"

The truthful answer was both yes and no, so she remained silent. His eyes ran over her, noting the tight jeans, the stretched, low-cut blue T-shirt, the straying strands of black hair. "You admit to the world you're my woman now, do you?"

"Not to the world," she answered sharply. "Anyway, I had no choice, did I? I mean, if I hadn't agreed, you wouldn't have asked Dr. Mansfield to come and see Cassandra."

"Wouldn't I?" He took up her left hand, parting the fingers. "Does it annoy you that this hand is bare, and that I've refused to acknowledge our liaison with a ring, so that you could boast openly that you're Gregg Barratt's fiancée? Whereas instead you're just Gregg Barratt's woman?"

She snatched her hand away. "You've asked a lot of

questions, so there'll be a lot of answers." When it struck her that the truthful answer to them all should be yes, although to retain her self-respect she would have to lie by saying no, she took the only course open to her and bluffed her way out.

"We don't have a 'liaison,'" she attacked him, "nor do I ever want to boast, not about anything. As for being your 'woman,' it's all a big pretense, isn't it? You thought it up only to embarrass me, to—to use me."

"*Use* you? That's a new one. How am I using you?"

It was a wild guess, but it served to keep his mind from dwelling on the fact that she had not answered a single question. "To keep Lola Buxton in her place until she's legally free. When she is, I know you won't lose any time in getting me off your back so you can marry her."

He looked puzzled. "Did I ever tell you I intended marrying her?"

"Maybe not. But she told Cassandra." Tanis stared at the dry crushed twigs all around.

Gregg turned, pushing her down and leaning over her. "Would you believe me if I told you that when I said I wanted you as my woman in exchange for finding a top-class specialist, Lola didn't figure in my calculations?"

"Then exactly why did you trade my reputation for the services of a specialist?"

"Reputation?" He ran a finger lightly down her profile. "I didn't think women had such things these days. And as for that 'liaison' of ours, you seem regretful that it's not a genuine thing. We could make it real, Tanis." He was touching her now, with his own body, his hip against hers, his legs imprisoning both of her legs. His finger was burning a trail down her throat to the enticing hollow that her T-shirt revealed.

There the finger lingered tantalizingly, then moved again, down, down the valley between her breasts. It

paused and her eyes flickered open. In his eyes she caught a look of contemplation, as if he were assessing what her reaction might be if his hands became more audacious.

Her eyes shut tightly before his keen intelligence could home in on her secret wish that the so-called liaison between them could be made real; that he could go on and on, forcing from her the final surrender. There was a laugh from his throat as if her ruse to keep her secret had failed. It hadn't needed a certain look to tell him of her willingness to let him make her his. Her entire recumbent form, lying there waiting, waiting, had been sufficient.

As if tiring of playing games, he moved abruptly until his body covered hers entirely. It was not in her to lie there unresponsive while he took what he wanted—not when her feelings for him were so overpowering. Her arms wound around his neck. When his lips took hers lightly, parting them as carefully as a botanist coaxing open the bloom of a rare plant, she did not deny the invasion of his mouth.

His hand had made its way beneath her shirt, his palms leaving a tingling trail over her midriff to rest on her ribs. When his thumbs found and stroked the hardening pink tips of her breasts, exciting her to a pitch where her body of its own accord arched against the angled hardness of his, she became aware that his claim that their liaison could be made a reality was more than true. It would take no time for the yearnings of her body to overcome the objections of her mind, causing her to yield to his demands without reserve.

There was the steady clip of horses' hooves on the hardened mud of a nearby horse trail. As the sounds came nearer, and the deep breathing of the animals together with the creak of leather could be heard, Gregg eased away, withdrawing his hand and resting on his elbow, smiling down into Tanis's wide, still vulnerable eyes.

Her hand went to her lips, which had until the interruption been utterly possessed by Gregg's. She felt already as though she belonged to him, but a glance at the half-veiled mockery in his smile told her that the feeling was an illusion. He had merely been indulging himself by taking from the girl beside him as much as she would give.

The clip-clop of the hooves and the chatter of the young girls on the horses' backs drifted into the distance. Still Gregg said nothing. Tanis gazed up into his face, loving the black, quirking eyebrows, the curving angles of his cheekbones running down to a thrusting, inflexible chin. His nose came to a decisive point from which his nostrils curved to meet the grooved lines running down to the corners of his sensual mobile mouth.

She wanted to reach up and hide a hand in his deep brown hair, to test his cheeks and jaw for bristle shadow. Once again she wanted to pull him down so that she, this time, could initiate a kiss, one she would give him as she had not so long before.

"You look," he mocked her, "frustrated. As if—" his gaze dwelt on tousled hair, her classic nose, her long curling eyelashes "—you hadn't had enough."

Her head turned away. "You're bordering on the crude, Dr. Barratt," she quipped. "A man of your position in life should be above such things."

"Ah, but—" a finger skimmed over her full pouting lips, ran lightly across her throat from one ear to the other "—as I've warned you before, underneath that particular man is a very different person—an animal likely to leap at your beautiful throat."

Rolling onto her side, she gazed at him, her eyes half-shut and provocative. "Know what, Dr. Barratt?" she murmured huskily. "I can be an animal, too, if the situation requires it."

Her hand had strayed to his cheek where earlier she

had wanted to place it. The pads of her fingertips ran downward and his hand came up to grip her wrist.

"Is that 'come on' or 'keep off'? Either way, it has the same effect on a hot-blooded male." He moved across her again, imprisoning both her wrists. He was rougher now, his mouth edging toward the brutal, the male drive of him unmistakable against her. His hand grew more impatient with her T-shirt, pushing it upward and fastening with a touch of cruelty on the yielding softness, molding, compressing with demanding insistence.

Tanis felt herself slipping, slipping down into a mist of nonresistance and absolute surrender. Something was wrong, a voice shouted inside her head. There were too many uncertainties, too many problems unresolved.

"Too public," she heard someone say, and realized it was herself.

"Okay—" hard lips hovered "—we'll get back to the car and carry on there."

By now she was turning and twisting. "That's not private," she argued fiercely. "There'll be other cars parked there now."

"Tonight, in your bed—or mine. Take your pick. Whichever place, I'll make you my woman good and true and no other man who comes after will have any doubt that you've been mine."

"Oh, God, Gregg," she choked, "what are you saying? You're crazy, you know that?"

He was still weighting her down, his head poised above her, his face like a mask, his jaw ridged like a jutting rock. "I've kept my side of the bargain. Keep yours. You say you're mine, but touches, kisses—against the real thing they're puny, like a sand castle compared with the might of Everest." His voice softened. "You're my private summit to achieve. I'll conquer you, my lovely bright eyes; I'll make you so much mine you'll feel lost without me."

It was a vow that inspired both fear and elation. She wanted to be swept away on the raging torrent of his words, but she grasped at the safety rope of sanity her subconscious mind had tossed her. It told her to ask the impossible.

"Give up Lola," she told him. "Discard her publicly. Make me your fiancée. Give me a ring. Let the world know I'm the one you're going to marry. *Then* I'll be your woman—in every way you want."

Breathlessly she awaited his reaction. When it came, it contained more amusement than anger. Thankfully, she relaxed.

"Those barriers of yours," he said, "those clearly defined boundaries you talked about before—they're getting in the way, Tanis." He picked up her left hand. "Everything tidy, in its place. So you want an engagement ring to calm your conscience, to let you face the world, head high, the conventional way. A man's ring, neatly gift wrapped, tied with pink ribbon and a label announcing, I belong to Gregg Barratt—Official. Well, my sweet, I've got news for you. The answer's no."

Then I won't be your woman. The words came into her head. She should have spoken them but they would not come. The reason was simple. She wanted to be Gregg Barratt's woman. At that moment, too, she wanted to be back in his arms, but he did not touch her.

At last she lay back, her hands forming a pillow, her knees bent. The gorse rustled, the heather whispered, the trees stirred and it was as though the past was surrounding her again. Raised voices of visitors became the shouts of kings and princes hunting deer, badgers, foxes and wildcats.

The clomp of horses' hooves changed into the clangs and hammerings from ancient furnaces and forges. In her dreamlike state she imagined they had returned, rising from the remains discovered in recent decades.

"Tanis?" An arm was pressing across her. Her name

spoken over her head had her drifting back to the present day. She stared up at the speaker, whose head was outlined against the blue of the sky. Fleetingly she saw him as a romantic, ruthless figure from ages past, fine, upstanding and perhaps with royal blood, merciless in his dealings with those who merited censure, compassionate with others who required gentler handling....

The vision passed and she saw him as he really was: a present-day man but possessing that ruthless, primitive streak of which he had so often warned her.

"Ring or no ring," he was saying, "this woman is mine. One day I'll take her."

CHAPTER EIGHT

"I'VE HAD TWO VISITORS while you've been out," Cassandra greeted them on their return. Her eyes shone and she was more animated than Tanis had seen her since before her accident.

"Both men, I assume," Gregg commented dryly without removing his arm from Tanis's waist.

Cassandra nodded. "Russell." Tanis glanced with surprise at Gregg on hearing her sister use Russell Mansfield's first name.

"And Frankie?" Tanis hazarded.

"Yes, Frankie. What do you think? He brought me flowers. Frankie and flowers! They just don't go together, do they?" she rejoiced, indicating the vase in which Mrs. Casey had arranged the colorful blooms.

"And what did Russell bring?" Gregg asked, smiling.

"News. Gregg—" a small frown appeared "—he wants me in the local hospital tomorrow, Sunday. Does that mean...well, that there's something seriously wrong and—"

"Not at all." Gregg strolled toward her, taking Tanis with him. "To a medical man, Sunday is just another day. Is there any reason why you shouldn't go?" Raised eyebrows turned to Tanis.

"None at all," Tanis answered. "At least things are moving, Cassie, which is what our efforts to raise money have been about, haven't they?"

"I mentioned fees," Cassandra said uncertainly, "but Russell said, 'Don't be silly,' and wouldn't discuss it."

Gregg laughed and Tanis felt the ripple of muscle as his ribs and waist moved against hers. She wanted to pull away and press closer at the same time. If only he weren't so attractive, if only his lovemaking was not such a seductive, sense-confusing thing. . . .

With reluctance she disentangled herself from Gregg's arm. "I must collect things you'll need. Did he tell you, Cassandra? Slippers, dressing gown—"

"Stop panicking, my love." Gregg's hands linked around her waist and his dark eyes met hers. "I can give you a list. It's all quite simple. She's not going for a prolonged holiday in a top-class hotel."

"I wish I were," Cassandra said sadly. "On the other hand—" she brightened "—when it's all over I'll be back to what I used to be, won't I, Gregg?" He did not answer quickly enough for her. "Won't I, Gregg?"

"Maybe even better," was the evasive reply, but it satisfied Cassandra. She turned to Tanis. "I told Frankie I'd be going to the hospital tomorrow and he said he'd come and see me there. He said to remind you about the work you and he are doing in London."

"Thanks, Cassandra. I meant to phone him before I left, but—"

"When he's been to see me at the hospital," Cassandra interrupted, "he said he'll come on here and talk about the decorations with Gregg. If he's allowed, he said," she finished with the kind of grin Frankie himself might have given.

It was early when Gregg took Cassandra, with Tanis beside her, to the hospital that was about five miles away. Gregg was well-known there since he, like Russell Mansfield, acted as a specialist there on certain days each week. It was not far from the roadside stand, Tanis remembered, at which she had displayed Cassandra's pictures and first met Gregg. And it was visitors to that hospital who had bought her friend Edna's flowers.

Cassandra was tearful when it came time for her sister

to leave. When Gregg appeared to take Tanis back, Cassandra listened seriously to his reassurances, knowing that he told her the truth.

"Russell will do his best for you," he assured her. "He told me he thought you were one of the prettiest girls he had ever met. There—" he smiled and squeezed her limp hand "—doesn't that make you feel better?"

"I know you said it only to cheer me up," Cassandra returned, glowing pink, "but it's done the trick!"

"WE'VE GOT ALL DAY," Gregg said, his hands on Tanis's hips as they stood in the living room, "to get to know each other."

"We know each other already," Tanis retorted, hedging.

"I know one side of your personality. You know one side of mine. There are other sides to each of us that, like most people, we've both kept hidden. And I demand to know everything there is to know about the girl who's my woman."

"No, Gregg, not that. I'm sorry, but—"

His hands slid to her waist, almost spanning it. "But yes," he said softly, "one day, before long, we'll complete our knowledge of each other."

He pulled her toward him until their bodies touched. "Put your arms around me," he commanded, and she did.

Then she was being cradled in his arms and her mouth belonged to him, just as all of her, if he cared to take it, was his to possess, despite her protests and refusals. As his hands held her breasts she knew that it was what she had been waiting for all the hours since he had made love to her in the forest.

He said at last, lifting his head, "We're spending the day in the enclosed garden."

"Where the swimming pool is going to be?"

He nodded. "We're going to pretend it's there, lying

at its imaginary edge, sunbathing beside its imaginary blue-tinted water. And we'll drown...in each other.''

Tanis knew she had to remind him and steeled herself for his withdrawal. "You haven't forgotten that Frankie's coming? About the decorating.''

Only a flick like a snaking whip that cracked across his gaze registered his reaction. Then his smile returned. "After visiting time, That's three o'clock to four today, which means he'll be here after four. There are a lot of hours between now and then.''

He released her. "Go upstairs and find a swimsuit. We'll dress for the part.''

"Like a play. After all—'' her eyes challenged "—we are only acting, aren't we?''

The narrowing of his eyes was followed by a sharp slap on her jean-clad rear. The blow stung and Tanis let out a small cry of pain. "Do as I say!" It was the man of authority speaking. Tanis obeyed.

The high-grown, neatly clipped bushes that surrounded the closed-in area caught the sun and held it. Tanis, lying on an inflated air mattress, felt the rays beating down on her bare skin. Her blue two-piece swimsuit was brief enough to catch the eye of any man, and the one beside her was no exception.

Opening her eyes, she glanced his way. She hoped he would attribute the sudden color in her face to the sun's rays. He said, holding out a plastic container, "You'll need this. I don't want to have to act the family doctor and treat you for a severe case of sunburn. It could spoil our fun.''

Tanis sat up, taking the sun lotion. "Fun? What fun?''

"Ours.''

She gave him a crushing glance, but by his answering smile she knew her censure had slithered off him, off the gleaming, lotion-lubricated tan of his skin. He watched

idly as she covered her exposed parts, and there was a mocking sensuality in his gaze.

It went with the rest of him, she thought, with the powerful shoulders, the sinewy ripples beneath the hard flesh around his waist. And the sensual pull of him held her like a rope holding a great ship by its moorings to the shore. Even when the time came for them to part, that link with him would remain, and nothing, no event or circumstances, would on her part sever it.

Their mattresses were side by side. A hand found Tanis's left hand and a shock tingled up her arm. His fingers seemed to be exploring hers. It was as if they had developed minds of their own and were searching for a ring, the ring that bound her to him. His reason must have prevailed over their blind instinct, for suddenly they were still.

Then the hand started caressing her arm as though its owner had a compulsion to touch her wherever he could reach. It was, she knew, a purely primitive force at work inside him, impelling the male in him to seek out the female in her. It was not who she was, she acknowledged with a sinking heart, but what she was—a woman—that was causing the restless movement of his hand.

When that hand crept over her stomach and lingered to stroke, a spasm of almost unbearable desire brought about a backlash from her brain. He must not be allowed to arouse her like this merely for his own pleasure. If this was what being his woman entailed, then it must end here and now. She jackknifed up and threw his hand from her.

"It's got to stop, Gregg—all this charade about you and me. I refuse to go along with it any longer."

A long-suffering sigh greeted her statement. "The barriers are up, yet I haven't even touched her!"

"Haven't touched me? You've kissed me and mauled me and—"

Now he shot up, his eyes darkening. "*Mauled* you? I'll show you what it's like to be mauled by a man!"

Before she knew what was happening, he was on her air mattress and his weight was crushing her. Thighs made abrasive contact with thighs, hipbones ground into hipbones and she knew for the first time the growing, relentless power of a man's desire. His hand was under her head, clamping it still. His mouth pried her lips open and he was making free of all the inviting moistness and honey sweetness it contained.

Then he shifted slightly to one side and on his face there was a purely male look that she had never seen before. Every part of him was experiencing and appreciating every part of her—and with the briefness of her two-piece swimsuit, little was left for his eyes to imagine or for his own half-naked body to fail to enjoy.

His hand came to life again, fastening lightly around her throat. An involuntary shudder coursed through her and she clawed at the hand, which merely tightened in resistance to her efforts. Then he bent low and his mouth again fastened onto hers, leaving both his hands free to roam all over her. A shoulder strap was eased down, and stroking fingers trailed the curves of her. Teasing lips found the thrusting pink tips of her breasts.

His mouth returned at last to hers. She tried shaking her head, to plead with him to stop, but the more she attempted to escape from him, the more deeply his mouth ravaged hers. The caressing became more potent as each skimming palm grew bolder, stroking across her stomach, her hips, her thighs. The moment she brought her legs into use to try to stop him, he was pressing down on her again, crushing the breath from her gasping lungs.

Now she knew how effective his preparations had been. Her body was on fire for him, loving the roughness of his chest against her, the urgent feel of his long, strong thighs. Her own desires took over and her ideas

of what should and should not be grew blurred as if she were wandering in a sea haze, then coming out into a burst of sunshine.

"*Now* I want you," he whispered. "Now, when your barriers are crushed to pieces. My love, it will have to be—"

"No," she answered in anguish, "not here, not where someone, anyone, might come along, interrupt, be shocked...."

She had reached his reason and he lay still upon her, his lips resting against hers. At last he moved away, back to his air mattress, lying, arm over his eyes, in complete stillness.

Tanis felt empty, denied—and guilty. She had allowed his advances; then, when she knew she should have said yes, she had let him down. He, unlike any other man she knew, had respected her wishes. And she wanted to cry until there were no tears left.

IT WAS SOME TIME LATER that he stirred. He had not been asleep, because now and then he had moved, rubbing at an irritation on his skin, wiping his brow with the back of his hand.

Tanis had never felt so inadequate. If she had followed her instincts she would have leaned over him, running a finger down his grooved cheek, pushing back his hair.

In refusing him and thus causing him heaven knew what anguish, she was too tied by her self-imposed rule of adhering to the path of convention to commit herself even to the man she loved. But something inside her whispered, *you would have been just one in a series.*

The fact that he refused to give her a ring, she reasoned, acknowledging her publicly as his wife-to-be, showed how selfish his motives really were. And there was Lola, always Lola, each day bringing her nearer to her divorce, which in turn brought her nearer to him.

Had it, therefore, been so wrong to refuse him? For him it would have been possessing just another woman. For her it would have been the first time, the most memorable, made with the greatest commitment, with her love for him the binding and most vital ingredient.

He sat up, shaking his head as if trying to free himself of torpor, of a dream. Had he slept, after all? He went back on his elbows and his head turned to her. It was as his eyes ran mockingly over her that she realized she had forgotten to replace her bra top and that he was greatly appreciating the fact.

Coloring, she adjusted it, then swung her eyes defiantly toward him. Still he looked her over. With a touch of derision he remarked, "You're the one I'll remember—the one who said no and by God, did you mean it!"

Part of her was intensely relieved that his good humor had not deserted him. The other part rebelled at the careless way he had referred to what had so nearly taken place between them. How would he have regarded her by now if she had allowed him the full intimacy he had desired?

He rolled toward her, stroking back her tangled hair, touching her swollen lips with gentle fingers. "But I admire you for it, respect you for it—and love you for it. Now, how's that for a man who's just been put in his place more firmly than any woman has ever dared to do before?"

Tanis joined in his laughter and happiness welled inside her that his integrity was such that he did not hold her refusal against her. Soon George Casey appeared carrying a picnic table, followed by his wife, who covered it with dishes and food.

They ate their meal as if they were sitting at the side of a swimming pool and laughed with each other about the splashing they pretended to hear of someone diving, about the gleam of the sun on imaginary water and how

they would race each other from one side of the pool to the other.

Afterward, somnolent with food and the sun's warmth, they lay side by side for some time in silence. A hand moving and capturing hers created a shock wave along the nerves of Tanis's arm. Her head rolled sideways to meet Gregg's smile, but only his relaxed profile greeted her.

This man she thought, looking at his sweep of jaw, his full lips and dark brows, was so well respected by his assistant and subordinates that they ran around before his visits to the hospital wards making sure that all was neat and in impeccable order for his illustrious eyes to rest upon. Yet he was here lying beside her, grasping her hand, making her pulses race, her instincts strain for her to be his mate in every primitive sense of the word.

Had her finger muscles tightened involuntarily on his to make him turn toward her and search her curving mouth, her large, wondering eyes? And had it been encouragement on her part that caused him to half rise, slide an arm beneath her and tug her across to share his air mattress.

Then whose initiative was it that made him ease her against him so intimately that their legs entangled, thigh between thigh, foot curling around foot, soft breasts to the wall of his chest? Did it matter, she thought bemusedly, as her forehead pushed into his neck and her fingers spread widely over the curling dark chest hairs. They were lying side by side, entwined like lovers satiated after making love. Except that they had not made love. . . .

Tanis thought she had slept and had awoken to find she was on her back, still beside Gregg, while he stared, arm under his head, into the cloud-flecked blue sky. "Gregg?" she asked. "Am I doing the job of being your woman to your entire satisfaction?"

His smile was quick, his finger reaching across to

press the tip of her nose. "No, you minx, and you know it. There's a hell of a lot more to being a man's woman than just lying in his arms and cuddling up to him like a kitten."

Her five fingers walked along his collarbone, diverting to explore his neck. "I'm sorry, Gregg," she whispered, "I can't let any man break through my barriers, until—unless. . . ." He did not help her. "So, you see, much as I love you. . . ." Her breath was a swift gasp as she played back to her scandalized ears the words she had just spoken.

He half sat, sideways. His eyes blinded her like twin midday suns. "She loves me. She says she loves me!"

Tanis was up and away, running, racing around the tall hedge to the lawn that was overlooked by the house. In sight of his housekeeper, he couldn't—he wouldn't. . . . A glance over her shoulder told her he was coming up fast. She skirted the lawn sprinkler and made for the patio doors.

A shock of ice-cold water over her back from head to foot had her gasping and twisting to see if she had knocked the sprinkler flying after all. But she saw it was Gregg who had seized the rotating sprinkler with both hands. He was gaining on her, intent on drenching her with it.

Her shrieks of "No, please," and "Stop, oh, stop!" had no effect. As the mechanism moved, it drenched him, too, but he plainly did not care. Her hair was saturated, covering her eyes. Her face dripped, her entire body ran with rivulets of water. Her brief two-piece outfit was soaked and clung as if she had indeed been swimming. He, too, was soaked but he seemed to be reveling in the fact.

"She loves me," he kept saying, "she's just said she loves me. By heaven, this will cool her ardor."

Mrs. Casey came to see what was happening, smiled and went away. George, her husband, emerged from the

rose garden to discover why his sprinkler attachment seemed to have been moved. He summed up the situation and like his wife discreetly disappeared.

Tanis turned and ran toward Gregg, using her arm to protect her eyes. She reached him and tried to wrench the sprinkler from him. It was heavier than she had realized and as she tugged she tripped over the rubber hose and sprawled full-length at his feet.

Gregg lowered the sprinkler to the lawn and flung himself beside her, turning her and dragging her into his arms. The sprinkler's jets reached out, swinging around toward them. As their lips met in a mutually passionate fusing, they were drenched again from head to foot.

For the second time they became entwined one with the other and Tanis could taste the ice-cold water from Gregg's ruthlessly exploring mouth. The saturation of their bodies, meeting and interreacting, increased their shared ardor and heightened the pleasure each was giving the other.

"It seems the proverbial bucket of cold water is insufficient to put out the fire." The words were uttered in a falsely tolerant tone. Behind the words, spoken with hauteur by a woman, was a hint of raging anger. "It's plain, darling, that when I told you to enjoy yourself before we married, you took me literally."

Gregg rolled away from the girl in his arms. He cupped his hand to his mouth and shouted, "George, switch off the sprinkler, will you?" A few moments later the water jets faded to nothing. Gregg stood, pushing back his dripping hair.

Turning, he looked down at Tanis, who still lay on the lawn. His fists were on his hips, his long, strong legs apart. "Look at her, the abandoned hussy. She told me she loved me, then ran away. I had to put her fire out somehow. But—" he pretended bewilderment and scratched his head "—I seem to have fanned the flames instead. Then I caught alight." A shoulder lifted and his

grin turned mocking. "What could I do but merge our fire until we—almost—got our fingers burned."

"So I arrived just in time to save your honor, Miss Foster," Lola Buxton sniped. "Assuming, that is, that your honor is still intact."

Tanis started to rise, then colored to see that one shoulder strap of her bra top had slipped, revealing a tantalizing glimpse of silky soft curves. Tugging the shoulder strap into place, she stood beside Gregg. He was still smiling, but now there was mockery in his eyes.

"If it is," he remarked with a touch of malice, "it's not for want of my trying to take it from her."

"Towels, Dr. Barratt, Miss Foster?" Mrs. Casey came across the lawn.

With the large bath towel covering her down to her knees, Tanis felt less at a disadvantage in relation to Gregg's glamorous visitor. Anger lurked inside her. Whether it was against herself for telling of her secret love, against Gregg for taking their relationship onto such an intimate footing and then letting his fiancée know about it, or against Lola Buxton for interrupting one of the most passionate embraces she had exchanged with Gregg, she could not decide.

"When you can tear yourself away from Miss Foster, darling," Lola Buxton said, sinking gracefully onto a white-painted garden chair, "I would like your advice on one of your patients."

His attention was caught at once, as she must have known it would be. "Which one? Mrs. Harrison?"

"How did you guess, darling?" Lola's smile was slow and inviting. "What a wonderful man you are—one minute acting the lecherous womanizer, the next being the real you, the fantastically clever surgeon."

"Do I cringe or bow at that feline comment?" Gregg queried sardonically. "I'll be with you in a few minutes." He turned to Tanis, his towel now draped

around his neck. His hand went out. "I'm going to change. Coming, darling?"

Tanis's hand went willfully on its way to his, despite the storm raging in her head. Darling, he'd called her, just as Lola had called him darling. Spoken as lightly as they had used it, the endearment meant nothing.

"Don't get too attached to my fiancé, Miss Foster." The words of advice came wafting on the spring breeze. "Enjoy your affair with him, if you like, but remember he's mine. Never in a million years will he be yours."

Unable to vent her fury on the speaker, Tanis turned it onto the man who held her hand. "Did I once say you had integrity?" she flung at him, knowing Lola was by now out of earshot. "Cancel that, will you? You may be a brilliant surgeon, but as a man you're a rotten, no-good cheat!"

Snatching her hand from his, she dived into the house and raced upstairs.

CHAPTER NINE

TANIS TIED THE BELT of her yellow button-front dress. It was sleeveless and low-cut to catch the sun. Like most of her clothes, it was attractive but inexpensive and its color contrasted well with the near black of her hair.

She wandered to her bedroom window, which overlooked the area of the garden where Lola sat, her white-sandaled foot moving in irritation at her neglect. Tanis knew that her own dress came nowhere near in style to Lola Buxton's outfit.

It was a one-piece cat suit, with plunging neckline, minute sleeves, the slacks section hugging her hips lovingly. Around her waist was a wide elasticized belt of emerald green. Her shoulder length red hair contrasted with everything else.

"Envying my fiancée?" The challenging words came from the doorway, and Tanis swung to glare at the speaker. He leaned on his shoulder against the door frame. He was dressed in a cream linen shirt and light brown casual slacks. He went on, "She has a lot to recommend her, I admit." He lifted himself upright and strolled toward the window. ":Good looks, fine figure, intelligence." He faced Tanis and his amber eyes mocked her. "Experience."

Tanis reared mentally, like an enraged horse. "Experience? You're praising her for that when you know I haven't got it? If that's what you want in your women—in your *woman*—then I'll go all out to get it."

He looked calmly into her outraged eyes. "How do you propose to do that? You're not the sort to sleep

with a man for the sake of it. I've learned that much about you. And it's rather a drastic step to get yourself entangled in a loveless marriage just to gain the experience you lack.''

''Isn't that what your fiancée's done?''

''I doubt whether it was loveless at the start. You see, her husband, as he still is, is a good friend and colleague of mine.''

''He's a doctor?''

''Like me, a specialist. His name's Angus Buxton.''

''And you've taken her away from him?''

He smiled into her horrified eyes. ''Now come on, Tanis—you know enough about me now to know the answer to that question.''

The anger went out of her. Such emotional tangles were way beyond her. ''Other people's problems, the way they mess up their lives—'' she shook her head ''—as though they had no control over their own destinies....'' She sighed, turning to the window. ''She's divorcing her husband, yet look at her—so calm and uncaring.'' She turned to Gregg almost accusingly. ''Hasn't she any feelings?''

''Is it my fault if she hasn't? I'm not responsible for her character.''

''No, but you intend to marry her, knowing what she's like. Your fiancée, you called her.''

He shrugged. ''A convenient term by which to refer to her, purely in private. The rest of the world knows us as 'just good friends.' ''

''She knows differently.'' Tanis stared out. ''You're hers, she's just told me. You heard her. You didn't contradict her statement. So where in all this mix-up do I come in?''

Gregg merely smiled. He pulled her to face him, linking his hands around her waist. ''A man needs a woman like you when he's got a female like Lola Buxton in his life.'' Tanis tried to twist away, but he pulled her

against him. "A woman who's vibrant and responsive and eminently desirable. With eyes big and brown, their keen intelligence spiced with deliberate provocation; and a look from them able to arouse a man's primitive instincts."

He tipped her chin and held his lips just out of her reach. The brush of his breath on her face, the hovering lips, maddened her.

"And what's more," he went on, "who's told me she loves me."

"I don't, I don't love you. It—it was a slip—a slip of the tongue. And I don't deliberately provoke—"

"As pleasant a Freudian slip as I can think of. And you do provoke, my love. Look at you now—drawing away so that I have to chase that mouth."

"I'm not—" What was the use of telling him that her head was moving backward to escape the power of his lips, in a movement almost of self-preservation?

When the kiss came, it was such a relief that she gripped his shoulders, involuntarily urging him closer, in her ecstasy sliding her hands up to rake through his hair. In pulling away she had drawn him down, leaving the way open for him to push her backward until she hung helplessly over his arm.

His other hand made free of her body, forcing a way in between the buttons, finding the essential femininity of her, plundering and near barbaric in his arousal of her to meet and satisfy his seemingly insatiable demands.

At last he lifted her, yet pulled her against him. "That's how I treat the woman—the real woman—in my life. And that's just the aperitif. There's more, much more, to come."

Her cheeks felt on fire, her body part of that conflagration. She would not be burned out by him!

"You're insulting me, calling me your woman, yet calling Lola Buxton down there your fiancée."

His arm dropped away and she swayed, feeling cold and discarded. "You want to go, to return to your old life, and we'll never meet again?"

There was a pain like a knife being plunged into her heart. He didn't care; just like that he'd let her walk out of his life. Slowly, slowly, her head nodded, but she stayed right where she was.

After a desperate struggle she whispered, "I can't leave you, Gregg, I can't. And what's more, you know it."

Her feet took her to the door. Glancing back, she saw that he was watching her, his eyes narrow and speculative, his mouth unsmiling.

TANIS WANDERED AROUND THE LIVING ROOM, picking up a newspaper and replacing it almost immediately. Nothing could hold her interest.

When would Lola go? When would Frankie come? The sunshine beckoned, fitful now. Tanis wandered out and stood at the edge of the lawn where only about half an hour earlier Gregg and she had lain entwined.

Now his entire attention was focused on Lola. He was listening to her every word. Was it their mutual interest in their work that was making Gregg lean toward her so closely, or was it that he could not resist her attractions, the perfume she wore, the occasional flutter of her long dark lashes as she talked?

The surge of jealousy that Tanis experienced at the sight of them, so oblivious to everything around them, brought in its wake a savage resentment that had her running to greet Frankie at the sound of his voice talking to Mrs. Casey inside the house.

He stood a little uncertainly at the open doors leading from the living room into the garden. He saw Gregg and his companion, then looked at Tanis.

"You've got company. And a rival, from what I can see."

Tanis contrived a tossing movement of her head. "Gregg means nothing to me."

"He doesn't? That's not what I heard from Cassandra this afternoon."

"Then the next time you see her you can enlighten her, can't you?" She seized on the subject of Cassandra as a means of taking his mind off Gregg and his visitor. "How is she?" Tanis asked eagerly.

"Chirpy. They've gone to work on her already. She's had a couple of X rays, which they're now waiting for the specialist to examine. He won't be in until tomorrow."

"Does she want me to go and see her again today?"

"Not to worry," Frankie said easily. "I promised to call in on my way home from here."

"You're being very good, Frankie."

For the first time Tanis saw him look just a little embarrassed. "She's a nice kid. When she can walk again, maybe we can get together like we did before."

"Don't break her heart a second time, Frankie. Next time you've got to mean it."

"Okay, okay, I'll mean it." He looked at Gregg again. "Who's the bird of paradise sitting beside him?"

"Her name's Lola Buxton. She works with him at the London hospital he's based at. She's in the middle of divorcing her husband."

"And, from the look of it, chasing her next one."

Something twisted underneath Tanis's ribs. Her fight for breath was almost a gasp. "Somehow I don't think Gregg's that easily caught." *But she's almost got him, hasn't she,* a spiteful voice muttered inside her.

Frankie looked at her, eyebrows raised. "So it's just as well, isn't it, that you're not trying to catch him."

"Come on," Tanis said irritably, "they know you're here."

Gregg rose the moment Tanis appeared. He nodded at Frank, then made the introductions. Lola's eyes

darted from Frankie to Tanis. "Your boyfriend, Miss Foster?" There was hope in the question.

"Cassandra's," Tanis answered shortly.

"Disappointed, Lola?" Gregg gibed, smiling at Lola's angry flush. He asked Frankie, "How's the patient?"

Frankie told him and Gregg nodded as if he expected it. "Russell couldn't make it down here this afternoon. He'll be at the local hospital tomorrow."

"It'll be diagnosis day, then?" Frankie inquired.

Gregg nodded again. "We'll know the best—"

"Or worst," Lola put in spitefully.

Frankie half turned away. "Proper little optimist," he murmured so that only Tanis could hear. "Well," he said overheartily, "could we start on our tour of the house? I told Cassie I'd call in when I'd finished here."

Tanis glanced at Gregg in triumph. *See*, she wanted to say, *I haven't taken him away from her.*

Lola accompanied them on their walk from room to room. Frankie rose to the occasion, having, Tanis sensed, judged the intellectual rating of his audience to be higher than average. He talked expansively about color pyschology and the research that had taken place in recent years on the importance of a correct color environment.

"Hospitals, offices and restaurants are carefully color schemed these days," he informed them, "to promote the right atmosphere for healing, working, eating and so on."

Gregg listened impassively, Lola wide-eyed with surprise as she heard the young man she had plainly dismissed as of below-average intelligence explain the many different aspects of interior decoration that until then she had never even though about. He talked about color combinations.

"Your choice can't be wrong," he went on, "if it pleases you. There aren't really any rules. But like

anything else, the fashion of the times plays a part."

As they moved around, Lola began to dominate the discussion, telling Gregg what she would like on one. room and what she would not be able to tolerate in another. Gregg considered her choices, with Frankie joining in, until it became a triangular conversation from which Tanis found herself to be entirely excluded.

If Lola wanted to put me in my place, Tanis thought bitterly, *then she's certainly succeeded*. When the group reached the bedroom she herself occupied, Lola's ideas were in full spate. Not one of the others turned to Tanis herself and asked if the ideas pleased her.

"Of course," Lola commented, smiling patronizingly, "by the time I move in here, Miss Foster and her sister will have gone."

Tanis gazed at Gregg in alarm, but his only reaction was to raise his eyebrows and shrug as if shaking the problem from his shoulders. A retort spring to Tanis's lips; a futile anger had the blood singing in her ears. Then she turned away, keeping her fury on a tight rein.

What was the use, she asked herself, when it was obvious that Gregg condoned Lola's comments? She and Cassandra would have to resign themselves to the fact that in a few months they'd be forced to find themselves a new home.

Downstairs again, Gregg and Frankie discussed wall coverings and color schemes. Lola had her say here, too. Tanis wandered to the window, only half listening, gazing into the garden and regretting with all her heart that she had in an unguarded moment told Gregg she loved him.

"You've taken a note of my choices and preferences, Mr. Anderson?" Lola asked imperiously before she left.

"Are you paying for the cost of the decorations, Miss Buxton?" Frankie asked with a flash of his customary impudence.

Lola turned a deep red, plainly taken aback by the sudden switch to the personal level from the professionalism that Frankie had been displaying. The woman, Tanis decided, suppressing a smile, had probably never been put in her place with such swiftness by someone whom she had clearly regarded as being of an inferior breed.

Tanis glanced through her lashes at Gregg, who was looking back at her with a faint dry smile. Why, she wondered, had he let his fiancée get away unchecked with such effrontery? Unless she really was at some future date going to become his wife?

Lola's arms wrapped around Gregg's neck and her mouth reached up to draw a passionate kiss from his. Tanis had turned away, unable to stand the sight of her in Gregg's arms.

Before leaving, Frankie reminded Tanis of the work still outstanding back in London. "Don't worry," she promised, "I won't let you down. I'll get there somehow."

"I'll take you to the nearest subway station each morning," Gregg offered. "But I can't be relied on to bring you home. My hours are unpredictable."

"Oh, I'll bring her back," Frankie stated. "I'll be coming this way to see Cassie in the hospital. By the time she's out of there, we'll have started on this place."

"Good," said Gregg.

Tanis thought, *Frankie really is serious about Cassandra.* Instead of quelling her fears as it should have done, it intensified them. How much was Frankie's new devotion based on real effection and how much on possibly false expectations of a complete cure?

Optimistic though she herself was of the outcome of Cassandra's treatment, there always lurked at the back of her mind the possibility that her sister might never return to the state of complete mobility she enjoyed before the accident. If that were so, what would happen to Frankie's devotion then?

TANIS LOOKED FORWARD each morning to the drive to London with Gregg. It lasted only just over a week, however, since the work in the area in which she had distributed the leaflets was soon completed.

Every evening of the second week Frankie took her home, then backtracked to the hospital, from which he returned to London. Every evening Tanis went to see Cassandra, too. She went alone because Gregg was rarely home until late, sometimes even staying a night or two in London.

When he was away, George Casey drove her to the nearest station and she would travel by train from there. It did occur to her that Gregg was trying to avoid her, maybe because her confession about her feelings for him had embarrassed him, although deep down she doubted this. Since he had so often told her that beneath the doctor layer of his character there existed the real man, a woman telling him she loved him would no doubt have acted as a fillip to his male pride.

Cassandra told her one evening that Dr. Mansfield had decided that although one leg was in a good state of recovery, needing an intensive course of physiotherapy to restore it to normality, the other required surgery. The sooner the better, she added.

"He said it's already been left too long."

Tanis, sitting beside the hospital bed, said, "We were saving money as fast as we could. Did you tell him that?"

Cassandra nodded. "He frowned and shook his head, as if he was sad—about our situation, I suppose. If you hadn't been selling my paintings in the rain and if Gregg hadn't come along when he did and saw you there, it would have been much worse, wouldn't it?"

Tanis could only nod.

Impulsively Cassandra seized her sister's hand. "I think he's wonderful."

"Who?"

"Russell Mansfield. He's a—a kind of dream man."

Her eyes had a faraway look. "I always did prefer fair-haired men."

"Hey, what about Frankie? He's brown haired. You've never grumbled about his hair coloring."

Cassandra frowned. "Well, no, but Dr. Mansfield's different." She closed her eyes. "Different in every way."

"Hero worship," Tanis warned, feeling, to her own surprise, a little apprehensive. "It's your age," she teased.

Cassandra's eyes flew open. "It is not! I'm coming up to twenty-one. I should know my own mind, my—" she smoothed the sheet "—my own preferences by now."

A bell rang, indicating the end of visiting time. "Yes, well," said Tanis, "when's the operation?" She stood up, putting the box of Cassandra's favorite chocolates on the bedside cabinet.

"Soon." Cassandra hung onto her sister's hand. "I'll be glad when it's over. But—" her eyes lifted, seeking reassurance "—with Dr. Mansfield doing the operation, it should be all right, shouldn't it? I really do trust him, Tanis."

"That's fine." She patted the hand in hers. "With luck, or should I say with Dr. Mansfield's skill, it should be the last, shouldn't it?" Cassandra nodded. "Then gradually the use of your leg should come back. Slowly, I expect, but—"

"I don't care how long it takes, just as long as I can walk properly again."

IT WAS THE THURSDAY EVENING of the second week in which Tanis and Frankie had completed their work in London. For two days Tanis had nothing to do.

"Let's have a break before we start on the Barratt residence," Frankie had suggested. "I'll arrive first thing next Monday. Okay?" Then he had driven off as usual to visit Cassandra.

Gregg had not returned home the previous weekend. Tanis found herself fretting, missing him so much that it became like a nagging pain. She told herself she was foolish, that he was almost certainly spending his free time with Lola and that he had forgotten all about the tenant in his house called Tanis Foster, whom he chose to call his "woman" when it suited him and ignored when it did not.

Cassandra was, as usual, pleased to see her. It seemed to Tanis that on that particular evening her sister was more than pleased. She had hardly seated herself in the chair beside the bed when Cassandra informed her, "The operation's the day after tomorrow. In a way I'm dreading it, but if it's successful...well, I won't look back, will I?" Her eyes pleaded for confirmation and Tanis, responding at once, nodded vigorously.

"With a man like Dr. Mansfield attending you, things *must* go right, mustn't they? I mean, he's so good at his work. Gregg wouldn't have consulted him about you otherwise, would he?"

Cassandra shook her head and settled back against the pillow. Her eyes moved sideways as if summing up her sister's mood. "Tanis," she said at last, "would you—could you possibly do something for me? It would mean the world to me if you'd agree."

A spurt of apprehension shot like a fountain from her tensed stomach muscles to her brain. Something was coming, something she was sure she would not like. Over the years she had given Cassandra everything she wanted. Was she about to pay the price for the indulgence now?

"I want you to stop Frankie coming to see me." Cassandra's hands clutched the bedclothes, as she waited for Tanis's answer.

Tanis tried not to let her panic show. "How do you propose that I do that? I can't control his movements. Anyway, he comes here because he wants to see you."

"But I don't want to see him. Not anymore."

Tanis tried to speak lightly. "What has he done to deserve this? Not kissed you enough?"

"I'm not fooling, Tanis. I—I just want him out of the way."

"You're not—you can't be serious about Russell Mansfield?"

"I've never been so serious about anything."

Tanis's mouth was so dry she wished she could drink some of the fruit juice on Cassandra's bedside table. "Has—has he said anything, Cassie? Dr. Mansfield, I mean."

"He can't, can he? I mean, I'm his patient. He mustn't give the slightest sign, not until I'm out of the hospital." She gazed unseeingly at the wall. "Sometimes he comes in at the end of the day just to ask me how I feel, and if the physiotherapy's helping my other leg. He doesn't say much, just stands there looking at me." Her head lifted from the pillow. "I can tell, Tanis. I just know he likes me, really likes me!" She subsided. "And I think he knows I like him back."

"So what do you want me to do about it?"

"Don't sound so sour, Tanis. All I want is for you to—well, to take Frankie off my hands."

"Look, Cassandra, I've done a lot for you in the past—"

"And I've appreciated it." Cassandra confided disarmingly. "Every single thing."

"But you must know that I like someone. I like him a lot."

"If you mean Gregg, Tanis, you're wasting you time. That Lola woman will be free soon. She's determined to get him. From the things she's said to me, there's no question about it. Gregg intends to marry her. She told me once he couldn't marry a woman outside his profession because he'd have to be able to talk to her in a

language she'd understand—*his* language, medical matters."

Tanis could not prevent the droop of her shoulders. Cassandra put out a hand and Tanis was compelled to cover hers fleetingly. *As if,* she thought, *Cassie needs the comfort, when I'm the one who's going to suffer the torment.*

"I still don't know, Cassandra. It's you Frankie likes."

"He likes you, too."

Tanis made a noncommittal movement. "He tries it on, we both know that, but not since he's known you won't be in a wheelchair for life."

Cassandra's eyes rounded. "That's just it, isn't it? If he really loved me my accident wouldn't have altered a thing. And what if—if the operation isn't a success? No, don't say it. We've got to face the possibility. What would Frankie do then?"

THAT LOLA WOMAN'S DETERMINED TO GET HIM. There's no question about it. Gregg intends to marry her. The woman he marries would have to talk his language....

Cassandra's words went around and around in Tanis's head all night and throughout the following day. *I want you to stop Frankie coming to see me... take Frankie off my hands....*

I haven't made any promises, Tanis reminded herself, *but I didn't refuse, either. And if,* she reflected, *I follow my usual custom of giving Cassandra everything she asks for, I'll give in to her this time, too.*

The question remained as to how she was to accomplish the act of taking Frankie off Cassandra's hands. Let him know by signs and actions that she was available, that she wouldn't repel his kisses, that she would allow him to touch her, caress her...? The thought filled her with horror. The one man she wanted to touch her was Gregg and only Gregg.

Since Frankie had not brought her home for the past two days, he had not visited Cassandra. He did not plan to do so, to Tanis's knowledge, until Monday, when he would be arriving at the house to begin work. It was with immense relief that Tanis realized the problem could be safely shelved for the next two days.

For some time she had been wandering listlessly around the house. She had told Cassandra she would need time to consider the proposition and would not be going to see her that evening. Mrs. Casey had volunteered to go in her place and Tanis had gladly agreed.

Since she had lived in Gregg's home, Tanis had not been in the room where the two of them had breakfasted together the weekend she had stayed there. Gregg had called it the morning room. To her it had seemed a place that offered comfort and relaxation; a place in which she felt she could be herself. She found it after opening and closing two or three doors.

There was no coziness about it now. Gregg had made it into an office, thus depriving it of most of its character. One of the armchairs had gone; so had the slender glass vases containing the flowers. The dining table remained, but its polished surface could not be seen for the papers, books and folders that covered it. A chair was drawn up to the table and a pen rested beside a pile of handwritten notes.

Among the notes were diagrams, explanations and more diagrams. It seemed they were part of a series of lectures for medical students. Did it mean that Gregg was not only a surgeon but also held some kind of academic post as a tutor, maybe even a professor?

Eagerly she sat down and pulled the textbooks toward her, flicking through them and lingering when something vaguely familiar caught her eyes. She had been under the impression that she knew quite a lot about her own body; how little she really knew was revealed to her

now. It was obvious that Gregg, being an obstetrician, knew all there was to know on this subject.

There were many passages in the notes, also, that were well beyond her comprehension. If only, she thought, she possessed Lola Buxton's knowledge and was able to talk to Gregg in the same way as she could, discussing new theories, improved treatments. If only she could reach him on the intellectual as well as the physical level, maybe she would be Gregg's wife-to-be instead of just his woman—yet she wasn't even that, really.

Tanis sighed, resting her elbow on the table and her head on her hand.

"Have you suddenly decided to abandon interior decorating and study medicine?" An amused voice came from the doorway.

"Gregg!" Tanis tensed guiltily. Her warm confusion seemed to amuse him even more. He came to stand beside her and at once her whole body was electrified with a stinging excitement.

Relaxed though he was, he still wore a classically cut suit, and the faintly aloof air of authority that, she guessed, set him apart from those who worked with him in the course of a hospital day. Feeling almost as abashed as one of the many medical students who no doubt followed him around, Tanis gazed up at him. Her smile was tentative and seemed to touch a chord deep within him.

His fingers tipped her face. Afraid that he would perceive the torment that had clawed at her for almost twenty-four hours now, she attempted another smile, but the anguish that was consuming her very soul stopped it in its tracks. In a few days would he hate her, she wondered.

For a moment he dwelt on the uncertainty that flickered in the wide brown eyes, then considered the well-shaped lips, but his words were less personal than his scrutiny.

He released her chin, saying dryly, "You wouldn't start your studies at that level," indicating the notes. "They're meant for final-year students."

"All the same," she rallied, determined to live by the moment and let the future do its worst, "I can understand it." His doubting frown cut her short. "Well, here and there." She grinned up at him. "Now and then. A word or two." He smiled with her. She patted her stomach. "I do know what I'm like inside. More or less. Well," she qualified, "I've seen diagrams." Was she talking his language? It seemed not, judging by his amused expression.

"Give it up, my love." How long would she be his love? He stroked her hair. "I know enough about the subject for the two of us."

But, she wanted to tell him, *there won't always be the two of us. Time is running out. But you don't know that.* Soon, if she agreed to Cassandra's appeal, it would be Lola to whom he would be referring when he spoke those two words. Wasn't that true anyway? It was Lola now and Lola tomorrow, all their tomorrows. She tore her mind away from what was to come and forced herself back to the present moment. And at that moment he was there, with her and no one else.

He removed his jacket, then loosened his tie, unfastening the top buttons of his shirt. Tanis watched him, fascinated. Sensitive as she was to everything about him, his actions spoke of an intimacy between them that was total. There was a twist of pain somewhere, telling her that such a thing would never be.

He dropped into the armchair, put back his head and closed his eyes. Tanis could almost feel the tension flowing out of him, leaving him free but filling her instead. The look of vulnerability about him, the need she sensed within him for an easing, if only temporarily, of the problems that troubled his mind, had her hands clench-

ing and her breathing momentarily checked as she fought to keep herself from running to him.

His arm extended slowly toward her, although his eyes stayed closed. She froze, not knowing how to respond. "Come to me," he said softly. She needed no second bidding.

She was pulled down by two strong arms, seated on his lap and cradled, held to him, his cheek on her hair. Her face was turned to him, rising and falling with the movement of his chest. She lay against him, malleable, compliant, inhaling the male scent of him, her arms encircling his body as far as they could reach.

The lean muscularity of him pressed into her arms' untried softness, the physical strength of him unyielding beneath her touch. At that moment she longed to be his woman in every sense of the word.

"It's been a long time," he said into the stillness. Tanis had never felt so close to the very essence of him, not even in the forest, nor even when they had kissed so passionately on the lawn in the sunshine.

"Look at me," he demanded, speaking low and intimately. His amber eyes sought the brown of hers. Desperately she clung to the present, refusing to let her fears show through. "Let me feast my eyes," he mused. "I want to saturate myself with you. With your sweetness and sympathy, your understanding, your transparent honesty. And," softly, "your loving."

Honesty, she thought, momentarily closing her eyes. *He doesn't know what's to come!* But she responded evenly, "You do believe, then, that I love you?"

He answered obliquely, his smile washed over with mockery, "Isn't that what a woman is for—to love her man?" Then, more seriously, "I do believe you love me."

The tightening of his hold disturbed yet excited. The life force was flowing within him again and it was communicating itself to her. But old habits asserted

themselves and she sought for something with which to distract him, doubting her own ability to refuse anymore what this man might demand of her. "Dinner's over long ago," she told him quickly. "Mrs. Casey's gone to see Cassandra. You were so late home. Are you hungry?"

Knowing him as she did, she reproached herself, she should have known better than to ask such a question. His tilted smile warned her of what was to come. "Why? Are you offering yourself to me—on a plate? If so, you'd have to whet my appetite first."

"No, of course not. I—"

His mouth lowered. "Like this." His lips homed in and fastened securely. Spontaneously her arms lifted to cross behind him, and she rejoiced in his possessiveness, in his attitude of taking what he deemed to be his. His caressing hand traced her inviting curves. It followed the outline of her hips and thighs, then moved higher, growing irritated with the T-shirt that stood between it and its goal.

With abandon she gave herself to his delving kiss. It so deprived her of her powers of reasoning that when at last his probing fingers found a way through and his palm fondled the enticements of her breasts, she had lost all wish to resist. She surrendered herself completely to the consuming fire that his stroking hand was creating inside her.

This might be the last time, she thought, clinging to him fiercely, *the last time he smiles at me, touches me, kisses me....* Did Cassandra know what she was asking, she wondered feverishly, responding unreservedly to his lips, now gentle, now hard and compelling.

When he lifted his head at last he asked, "What are you trying to tell me, sweetheart? Is there something you want of me? Do you want me to take you, make you mine entirely?"

Her eyes looked brilliantly up at him, alight with love,

with longing—and with a nameless fear that must, she knew remain her secret. She shook her head. "Just hold me, hold me, Gregg." She sighed, resting her head on his shoulder while her body tingled with the caressing touch of his hand as it still cupped her breast.

There was the sound of a key in the door. "Mrs. Casey's back from seeing Cassandra," Tanis whispered hoarsely. "Gregg—" she struggled to sit upright "—she might come in."

"First she'll go into the kitchen," he assured her, smiling. As he spoke, the footsteps made for that direction. "Time to make yourself presentable," he teased, "and look as if you're just another female and not my woman. And there's no doubt that's what you look like at the moment."

He lounged back, legs full-length and crossed at the ankles, watching her through narrow, reminiscent eyes. "I've a mind," he mused, "to take you to bed tonight. It's been cold there lately. It needs a woman's responsive and ardent body to fill the empty space—and my arms. Does the idea appeal, lady?"

While he talked, she tidied her T-shirt and pushed back her hair, straightening her skirt and closing the zipper. She stood beside him, leaning down to push back his hair, and he caught her hand, putting the back of it on his cheek.

"Gregg, oh, Gregg, I wish...." She saw the sideways glance, the curving mouth tinged with mockery. "Just how do you expect me to answer that, Dr. Barratt?"

He laughed at her sudden anger and pulled her down to place a kiss on her mouth. "I know how you would like to answer, but I also know what your answer will be."

He released her as Mrs. Casey tapped on the door. "Miss Foster? Oh, Dr. Barratt, I didn't know you were home." If there was a tension in the atmosphere, the housekeeper did not appear to notice. "Miss Foster,

your sister sends her love. Her operation's tomorrow and she says she can't have visitors the first evening, but on Sunday she'd love to see you. She says not to worry about her. She's not worried, I can tell you that. This Dr. Mansfield who's doing the operation—well, she thinks he's wonderful and can work miracles.''

Tanis laughed, but Gregg, who was standing now, his shirt refastened, did not laugh with her. "Russell can't work miracles, but there's no doubting his ability as a surgeon. If it's humanly possible to restore to Cassandra the full use of her legs, then he's the man to do it.''

"Well, I believe in him," Tanis stated, "as Cassandra does. I'm convinced that she'll walk normally again one day." She turned to Gregg. "Thank you for the part you played in securing Dr. Mansfield's services. If he doesn't mind waiting for a while for his fee. . . .''

"He's waived his fee," Gregg said shortly.

Mrs. Casey withdrew, saying, "Then he's a wonderful man, just as Cassandra said.''

Gregg pulled Tanis to him, his hands linked around her waist. "Tell me, if—heaven forbid—I ever had to perform an operation on you, would you have as much faith in me?''

Tanis gazed up at him, her eyes adoring, but she didn't care. "I'd put my life in your hands," she said simply, then reached up shyly to kiss him.

CHAPTER TEN

BREAKFAST WAS OVER and Gregg pushed back his chair. "I know it's Saturday, but I have work to do. Can you amuse yourself, sweetheart?"

Sweetheart.... Tanis reveled in the endearment, held it to her like the one surviving flower from a fading bouquet. Each hour until Monday, when her deception would have to start, was like a precious but fading bloom. She would need to cherish each one, lingering over it and doing her utmost to prolong its existence.

"I've got magazines and books to read. Gregg—" she went over to him "—would you mind if I sat with you in your study?"

He laughed and pressed the tip of her nose. "That's a strange request. May I ask why?"

Why? How could she answer, *because I want to make the most of my time with you, be with you every possible passing moment?* Her fingers flipped the pointed ends of his shirt collar. "I like the atmosphere in that room. That weekend I stayed, we had breakfast in there. Remember?"

"I remember." With relief she thought, *he's accepted the invitation.* "You can come in there while I'm working, if you want. But you must be as still as a mouse."

"A mouse isn't still. It scampers."

"You scamper, my sweet, and you'll find yourself across my knee."

"Right, I'll scamper." She smiled impishly up at him.

"You sorely tempt me," he growled, his hand fastening around her throat, "to abandon all thoughts of

work and take up a more comfortable position—on my bed. With you right beside me.''

Savoring the feel of his hand on her skin, she returned, ''Work first. Pleasure second.''

''I do believe the little minx is really trying to seduce me!'' His free hand joined his other at her throat and his mouth lowered to take a leisurely, thorough kiss.

It was difficult concentrating on the books and magazines that lay in a pile on the floor beside her as she occupied the armchair in the morning room. Gregg's dark head bent over his work, the complete absorption of his expression, the foolish sense of neglect that his withdrawal from her aroused. . . all made nonsense of the phrases that her eyes skimmed over but which her brain refused to unravel.

With an effort she forced herself to take in the meaning of the words and even became absorbed herself in one of the magazine stories. When Mrs. Casey knocked and entered, carrying a cup of coffee, she exclaimed, ''I've been wondering where you were, Miss Foster. I didn't expect to find you here.''

Gregg threw down his pen and rested against the chair back, stretching and yawning. ''I think she's trying to convince me of her hidden aptitude for medicine, Mrs. Casey. Last night I caught her studying my notes as if she had an exam to take today!''

Mrs. Casey laughed. ''Shall I bring her coffee in here, Dr. Barratt?''

''Why not? Did you think I wanted an opportunity to throw her out?''

The housekeeper laughed again. ''Well, you usually don't let even a fly share the room when you're working, let alone a human being.''

''And a woman at that,'' Gregg added. ''They're such a distraction, Mrs. Casey.'' He was standing in front of Tanis. ''Especially this one.''

The housekeeper bustled away with another laugh.

"Come on, Tanis, my devoted slave. Let your master relax in the only armchair the room possesses."

"I'm not your slave," she answered indignantly, but complying. "Nor are you my master."

"We could soon alter that," he rejoined softly. "A night sharing a bed. . . ." He sank into the chair. "Bring me my coffee, will you?"

Still faintly resentful, yet feeling a disturbing sensation creeping along her veins, she again obeyed his command, placing the coffee on a small table that she placed beside the chair.

"Now be my lapdog—" he tugged her down "—my domestic pet. Pets love being stroked, don't they?" His hand ran over her hair while his other rested lightly around her throat.

"Stop calling me names," she protested, but allowed his hands to remain.

Mrs. Casey returned and said, "Oh, my goodness, if I'd known I'd have knocked first." She handed the coffee to Tanis, who took it carefully.

"Don't worry," Gregg remarked calmly, "it's not my habit to treat my female students as if they were my women."

"I should hope not, Dr. Barratt," Mrs. Casey said, and left with a broad smile.

"No," Tanis returned, stirring her coffee, "it's only your lady tenants you treat as your women."

"Singular. Tenant. Woman. Get it?"

Tanis smiled, sipping the hot liquid, taking care that none of it spilled as a result of her precarious perch on Gregg's knee. For a while there was silence as they both emptied their cups, and the only sound was the clatter of cup on saucer. Putting hers on the table, Tanis asked a little hesitantly, "When would be the best time to call the hospital and ask about Cassie, Gregg?"

He consulted his watch. "Just after lunch. Why, are you anxious?"

"It's only natural, isn't it? I mean, any operation has its hazards."

"Maybe, but I assure you she'll be all right. The result won't be known for some weeks. You know that?"

Tanis nodded. "Thanks for the reassurance."

He smiled. "Think nothing of it. Tanis?" She looked at him. "Kiss me."

Her eyes widened, remembering the last time he had made the same request, except that this was an order. He was lying back, smiling lazily, arms hanging over the sides. There was a faint shadow around his chin and upper lip, as if he had shaved that morning in a hurry. His hair fell forward and his shirt was partly unbuttoned, revealing the other, darker shadow on his chest.

He was irresistible, dynamic, yet, as she knew to her cost, as elusive and beyond her reach as the summit of Everest. Even when she bent toward him and placed her lips on his, even when his arms came around her like steel bands, taking over the kiss and plundering her mouth, she knew that the tantalizing puzzle that was his real personality would never be hers to unravel.

IT WAS GREGG who telephoned the hospital to ask about Cassandra's progress. Speaking his name was like a magic key that opened all the necessary verbal doors.

His hand went momentarily over the mouthpiece. "She's doing fine," he told Tanis. "Just emerging from the anesthetic and asking for a drink." He spoke again into the telphone. "Russell? All goes well with the patient, I hear. Good. Fine. There's something I'd like to ask you."

Tanis crept away. Knowing that Gregg would not return to his work if she was still wandering listlessly around, she made her way upstairs to the bedroom in which Frankie had decided to start the decorating on Monday.

It had already been cleared of furniture by George Casey, and the fitted carpet had been securely covered, although Frankie had assured Mrs. Casey that they would provide their own protective sheeting.

There were one or two things Tanis knew she could do to help the preparation on its way. Returning downstairs, she found that Gregg had left the hall. The housekeeper confirmed that Dr. Barratt was working again, and did Miss Foster want to join him?

Tanis assured her that she did not. "Is your husband around?" she asked. "I'm thinking of making a start on one of the bedrooms and I wondered if there was any sandpaper available."

"Oh, he's got lots of that," Mrs. Casey said, and led her to the garden shed in which her husband was working. She repeated Tanis's request and George seemed pleased to oblige. He handed over some brand-new sheets of sandpaper, saying that that should keep her happy for a while.

Hoping to work at the lower levels since she had no stepladder—although she was sure George Casey could have produced that for her, too, if she'd asked—Tanis started on one of the two windowsills. Absorbed in her work, she did not hear the door open.

When two hands came down onto her shoulders, she gasped with fright. When the word "Sorry" was whispered in her ear, she let her arms hang loosely and held her head down as if to ward off a faint.

"I've been wondering where you were." He turned her around and looked her over. "Recovered from your fright?" She nodded and he commented, "Dressed in your best, I see." His eyes mocked the worn jeans and loose-fitting, faded pink-and-white-striped blouse.

"I'd hardly dress like a model to do this sort of work," she protested.

"True. You can make yourself look beautiful for this evening instead. Russell Mansfield's coming to dinner."

Later Tanis washed her hair, using the hair dryer Mrs. Casey had loaned her. Her hair hung in soft loose curls, one side brushed backward, the other curving over her forehead and her long sweep of cheek. Covering her hair with a shower cap, she took a bath and rubbed herself until her skin glowed.

The dress she decided on was an ankle-length evening gown of bronze satin. It had been bought some time before, but until now no occasion had arisen for her to wear it. Whether or not such a dress was appropriate, she did not care. Gregg's words had acted as a challenge. "Make yourself look beautiful," he'd said. Well, wasn't she doing just that?

The dress hung from a halter neck, plunging low into a rounded, revealing line just above her breasts. It followed her shape uninhibitedly, narrowing to her neat waist, wrapping around her hips and flowing from there to skim her gilt evening sandals.

The gold-colored earrings were her only jewelry. Her makeup was simple, highlighting her finely shaped eyebrows and long lashes and drawing attention to her perfectly shaped lips. Her eyes, her neat nose and the good bone structure of her face spoke for themselves.

As she descended the staircase, Gregg was leaving the morning room, a preoccupied look in his eyes. When he heard her and looked up, it was as if he could not believe what he saw. Yet no praise came from the line of his lips, no appreciation was reflected in his gaze. It was almost as if she had displeased him by doing her best to please him!

"You told me to make myself look beautiful," she protested as if he had attacked her verbally. At the foot of the stairs she paused, uncertainty making her hesitate. By the narrowing of his eyes it appeared that he had interpreted the hesitation as an attention-seeking device, a way of eliciting appraisal and praise, as would the model to whom she had referred earlier in the day.

"Which one of us will you be trying to seduce this evening?" he queried coolly. "You're dining with two bachelors. Tell me now, and if I'm not the one, I'll back out gracefully and let the other man win."

"Don't be so stupid, Gregg," she cried, hurrying to confront him. "Whom do you think I wore this dress for, did all this for—" indicating her hair and face "—if not for you?"

His expression altered subtly and he caught her to him, grasping her arms. "That, my sweet Tanis, remains to be seen."

"So you don't believe me! We're back to your old suspicions, your nasty hints about my morals." She felt like crying. Instead, she struggled to free herself. "So I'll go and take it all off, get back into my jeans and my old blouse, and then maybe you'll be happy."

His fingers pressed harder into her flesh, his hand spread out across the bareness of her back. His head moved slowly down, but Tanis turned her face away.

"No, no, you can't. You'll wipe off my lipstick. And your guest will be here any minute."

"I don't give a damn—"

The doorbell rang and Gregg cursed, pushing her away. "Russell's timing is poor. I'll have to tell him sometime."

All through dinner Russell's eyes kept straying to Tanis. At first it brought the color to her cheeks, but when she caught a look of curiosity rather than the admiration with which he had first gazed at her, then an occasional frown of puzzlement, she relaxed and took part more naturally in the pieces of conversation she could understand.

Once she glanced at Gregg, but saw no disapproval from him. Her behavior was as above suspicion as she could make it; she was trying to meet the two men on the intellectual level, thus, she hoped, drawing their thoughts away from her femininity and making them

treat her as—almost—an equal. The meal over, she rose, hoping fervently that when Russell Mansfield had gone, Gregg would not be able to accuse her of playing each man off against the other.

Russell exclaimed at the time and told Gregg that since he was driving back to London he should be leaving. He took Tanis's hand and assured her that all would be well with her sister.

Tanis's eyes lighted with happiness and she laughed with sheer relief. "I can't thank you enough," she told him. Telling them both good-night she climbed the stairs a little wearily to her bedroom.

There was a small cushioned chair near the window and Tanis sank onto it, letting her head hang back. The evening had been pleasant, but for some inexplicable reason, something of a strain. Gregg had been reasonable enough, letting his eyes linger on her shoulders, her face and now and then on the cleft between her breasts where they were revealed by the low-cut neckline.

But there had been an undercurrent, she was sure, although she could not pinpoint its source. Had it been in the occasional frowning glance that had come her way from Russell Mansfield? Had Gregg intercepted those glances and tried to interpret them?

They were still talking in the hall downstairs and even as Tanis listened they seemed to move back into the living room. When at last Russell left and his car engine started up and faded into the distance, Gregg still did not come upstairs to bed.

Tanis sighed, rubbed her eyes and slipped off her sandals. The mirror showed her an animated face, a less immaculate appearance than when the evening had begun. Fatigue had put shadows under her eyes, and the nagging worry that would not leave her added a look of anguish. Wasn't there time to back out, to refuse Cassandra's request, tell her to solve her own problems? That way she would keep Gregg's...what? Affec-

tion, admiration, desire? None of those was what she really wanted—his love. Lola Buxton had that, didn't she? After all, even Cassandra knew Gregg intended to marry the woman.

And, Tanis asked herself, could she tell a girl who had just been through an operation, had not yet even started to recover from it, and who had weeks to wait, anxiously, hopefully, until she knew the result, to find her own way out of a difficult situation? In the meantime perhaps losing the chance of getting the interest of the man with whom she seemed to have fallen in love and who, from what he had said that evening, appeared at least to admire her?

It was no use: she couldn't do it; she couldn't refuse her sister's request. If she herself were the loser.... She was, anyway, wasn't she? And wasn't she more of the stuff to take whatever was coming than Cassandra? In the past, ever since they had lost their parents, she had shouldered all the responsibility. She could—would—do it again.

She tugged at the bow of the halter neck of her dress, then reached around to pull down the zipper. It was when the front of the dress started to fall away that the door was flung open. Gregg stood there, his eyes like ice, his jaw clamped and thrusting. With his foot he swung the door shut and confronted Tanis, hands on his hips, head pushed menacingly forward.

Panicking, she held the dress to her, then with shaking hands managed at least to retie the bow at the back of her neck. "You can't come in here, Gregg. I'm getting ready for bed." She lowered herself to the chair.

"I can come in here when I damn well like."

"Now what have I done?" she asked, trying to hide her fear by injecting a note of irritation. "You can't accuse me of playing each of you off against the other. I wasn't trying for anyone's favors." He was approach-

ing steadily. "Could I help it if Dr. Mansfield kept looking at me?"

"Of course he kept looking at you, you beautiful
treacherous bitch." He reached out and pulled her
roughly to stand in front of him. "But not for the usual
reasons a man looks at a woman. He just couldn't
believe that someone so honest-looking, so intelligent,
so damned appealing could behave with such deceit."

"Deceit? Treacherous?" She shook her head, bewildered, afraid. "If you think—he thought I was out to
get him, then you're both wrong. Anyway, I'm not really your woman, Gregg. I'm just—"

"You're just a cheap little tramp. You're not my
woman, are you?" His hands on her arms were bruising
in their hold. "You're Frank Anderson's woman instead!"

"Not that again, Gregg!" Her heartbeats were almost
suffocating her. "I thought that his devotion to Cassandra lately would have convinced even you that *she's* his
girl."

"It was just a cover, wasn't it?" The more she struggled to free her arms, the tighter he held her. "A cover
for the affair he was carrying on with you."

"Wrong again, Gregg. You must believe me!
Gregg—" she was whispering now "—you're hurting
me badly. I can't stand it."

He ignored her pleas. "Wrong," he snarled, his eyes
searing like frostbite, "when Cassandra told Russell with
her own lips that Frank Anderson is now *your* boyfriend,
not hers? That he hadn't been to see her for the last three
days, which could only mean you had persuaded him
not to because you wanted him for yourself?"

Tanis's eyes widened with dismay. "Cassie told him
that?"

"Which means," Gregg persisted relentlessly, "that
you succeeded at last in doing what you'd intended right
from the start—to take him away from her."

Tanis shook her head thinking unbelievingly, *instead of waiting for my answer, Cassandra's gone ahead and as good as told Russell Mansfield that the way is clear for him to become more than friendly with her, if that's what he wants. But did she have to implicate me so devastatingly?*

How could she, Tanis agonized. Hadn't she thought of the consequences? No, she wouldn't. She'd been pandered to so much over the years—and by who else but the sister she had now let down so badly—that she would have assumed the answer to be yes and acted on that assumption. *I have only myself to blame,* Tanis reasoned miserably.

Aloud she told Gregg, "It's not true, what you've just said. And—and please let me go," she pleaded, her voice shaky.

"Let you go? You ask me to let you go when there's a bed, no one around to disturb us, and you—" he eyed her loosened dress "—with just a few bits of clothing in the way? It's the chance I've been waiting for—now that I know just what kind of a woman you are!"

He reached forward and tugged free the halter-neck bow. The dress fell forward again. In a swift movement he had her hands in one of his behind her back. With nothing to hold the dress in place, it fell to her ankles. He reached quickly to remove the one remaining item of clothing left. Now there were no barriers to hide her from his raking glance.

"Secondhand," he muttered, his eyes hooded as if estimating her potential, "but unbelievably beautiful. Since you've already been taught the rudiments of love-making by your man friend—"

She fought to free her wrists to escape from his insults and his scorching appraisal. He had other ideas. His free hand moved slowly toward her and she steeled herself for the first touch of him. He took her completely by surprise by bending and putting his lips to the

piquant rose pink points—and she caught her breath at the exquisite sensations the movement of his mouth against her was provoking.

There was a weakness at her knees and she knew that in a few moments her legs would refuse to support her. Gregg must have sensed that, too, because he scooped her into his arms and carried her to the bed. She was dropped onto it without ceremony and he threw himself beside her.

"Gregg," she protested weakly, "you can't mean it. You don't know what you're doing. You're making a terrible mistake. Please let me explain, please!"

His eyes were blazing now. The ice had melted but with anger, not the warmth of love. "How can I be making a mistake when my colleague hears the truth from your sister's own lips?"

"So without giving me a chance to defend myself," Tanis responded, moving agitatedly beneath the weight of him, "you've concluded that Cassandra felt so terrible about what I'm supposed to have done that she felt the need to tell someone, anyone? Dr. Mansfield was around, so she poured out her heart to *him*?"

"Not so impossible. Russell's a fine doctor. Maybe he felt his patient's recovery might be impeded if she went into the operating room with so much on her mind."

"And maybe," Tanis countered, "she wanted a way of telling him the field was clear for him?"

"A good try," he drawled, moving slightly to one side and looking with a touch of lustful insolence at her naked body, "but a worn-out theme. You can eliminate that. It goes against all medical ethics. It could get Russell struck off the register."

"You're so clever," she threw at him bitterly, making a vain attempt to hide her breasts with her arms, "you know all the answers. Well, there's one you don't know. I'm in the clear; my conscience is as white as virgin snow. Now will you let me go!"

Again he ignored the appeal and his lips lifted into a sneer. "Virgin?" he derided her. "You don't know the meaning of the word. Look at how you've responded to me every time I've made love to you." He moved his finger in an imaginary coil around her breast, pausing tormentingly at the point. "Look at you now. Naked, a man beside you and not a girlish blush to be seen." His smile was twisted. "And a look on your face that says, 'Take me, I'm yours—just as I'm any man's.'"

It's because I love you, she wanted to scream, but knew he wouldn't even listen.

His hands caught hers and forced them back above her head. Her hair spread over the pillow. She began to fight, to kick, to reach out to bite him wherever she could. If she was inciting him by her actions, she no longer cared. He avoided every lunge, dodged every snap of searching teeth.

At last he lowered himself onto her. Momentarily her hands were free as he pulled off his shirt in one quick movement. Immediately her nails dug into his shoulders, then moved to clutch and pull at his hair. He retaliated by doing the same to her.

"Let go," he commanded, and pulled until tears filled her eyes. She released him, but he did not repay the gesture. Instead his mouth twisted onto hers, forcing her lips open and exploring brutally, the moist interior. Then he cupped her face, continuing to exact his revenge from her mouth until small pleading cries from her throat told him she was beginning to surrender.

Against her will her body muscles slackened; her hands ran over his back, feeling the muscles, the thrusting shoulder blades. His mouth moved and went on a voyage of discovery, roaming her body, while his hands stroked and molded.

Consumed by the desire he had coaxed into a roaring furnace inside her, she found herself longing to surrender totally to the will of this man, the one man in the

world she loved. She felt her body lifting to maintain contact with his. Her lips sought his on their return journey from her tingling flesh.

When he rolled away from her, she could not believe it. It was like a physical pain. She was left with a passion-racked body, throbbing with unsatisfied desire; with a desperate wish to become one with him, only to be deprived and discarded with sneering contempt.

Shaking hands lifted to cover her face; her whole body trembled. "No," she pleaded, "no." Slowly she uncovered her face, only to find herself staring into his derisive eyes. "Why, Gregg, why? You must know what you've done to me. Now you've stopped." She sat up, holding her head, resting her forehead on her bent knees. "Oh, God, I can't stand it. I want you to take me." Lifting her head, she whispered, "I want to be your woman, Gregg."

He watched her silently, with hooded eyes and a rigid jaw. It was, she thought, almost as if he were enjoying her misery.

Rolling onto her side toward him, she pleaded, spreading her hand on his chest, "Make me your woman, Gregg." He lowered his head and kissed the tip of each breast. Hope lighted her eyes. "I'm not being brazen. It's because I love you so much, Gregg, I—I want to be part of you. I don't *care* if you don't love me."

He looked back at her, hard eyed, not moving.

She turned on him then, frustration, rejection, humiliation clamoring for an outlet. "You're a miserable, heartless swine!" Her eyes blazed. "I hate you. I've never hated anyone in my life, but I do now."

He watched her still, his lips taut, unforgiving.

A glimmer of modesty returned and she scrambled off the bed to reach for the dressing gown on the door. With shaking hands she wrapped it around her. Shock still had her in its grip, but there was nothing she could do about the trembling.

His eyes never leaving her, he said, as if considering the question, "Why did I stop?" He was so relaxed Tanis felt she could hit him. "To punish you for what you've done to Cassandra, unscrupulous little bitch that you are."

He swung to stand, pulling his shirt. "Despite all your self-righteous protestations of devotion to her, your constant denials of any form of involvement with Anderson, I now know the extent of your deception. I've heard the truth at last from your sister's own lips, through a third party whom I know I can trust implicitly." His slicing glance was like a whip. "I wouldn't take you now if you paid me."

With filling eyes she gazed at him, seeing his untidy hair, the deepening shadow around his cheeks and neck, the chest hairs that had so recently roughed her breasts, the merciless glint as he stared back at her and, worst of all, the twist of scorn around his mouth.

Her own lips still throbbed from the pressure of his. Her entire body felt as if it had been truly violated, yet he had, at the most exquisite moment and with calculated cruelty, thrown her aside.

At the door he turned. He must have seen the trembling lips, but he chose to ignore those, too. "I told you once," he said, "scratch my skin and you'll find the animal in me leaps at your throat." He smiled without warmth. "By your behavior over your sister's boyfriend, you scratched and drew blood. If I savaged you, you can't say you weren't warned. Sleep well," he commented as he shut her in, and malice made a mockery of the words.

REST ELUDED HER until dawn and the joyous birdsong wearied her into sleep. By the time she awoke it was late. Going downstairs, she found that Gregg had breakfasted and gone.

For this she was thankful, having been unable to bear

the thought of meeting his eyes across the table. She had known, of course, that the break would come. What she had not known was that it would come like this, with heart-tearing accusation and shattering brutality.

Finishing her breakfast and managing a convincing smile for Mrs. Casey, Tanis wandered into the entrance hall. One look at the morning-room door told her that Gregg was inside working. She sensed his presence before she heard the rustling paper. The bright morning called and she went out through the kitchen door, exchanging a few words with Mrs. Casey.

The fountain spurted high, dropping in a wide curve and causing endless circles to form and drift, to merge with the calmer water. Once her happiness had fountained high and joyously, when she first knew she loved Gregg, went to the forest with him, laughed with him and received his kisses with abandon.

Why had she let herself forget that constantly in the background there was another woman, one who had a much greater claim on Gregg's attractions and love than she would ever have? Right from the start she had known of Lola's existence, yet she had allowed herself to be fooled by circumstances, and Gregg's lovemaking, into thinking that in the end Gregg would realize his love for her and give up Lola.

It was just after coffee time that Lola herself appeared. Tanis had drunk her coffee while sitting on a garden chair; Gregg had had his alone in the morning room. Lola, having slammed her car door, wandered into the garden, plainly expecting to find Gregg there. Seeing Tanis sitting alone, she nodded unsmilingly and made for the kitchen. Tanis heard Mrs. Casey telling her that Dr. Barratt was busy working, and that she doubted if he wanted to be disturbed.

"Oh, he'll let me in," Lola claimed, and a door opened. "Darling," Tanis heard, "you don't object if *I* come in, do you?"

The answer must have been an invitation to enter, since the door closed and there was silence. Was it only yesterday, Tanis wondered, that she herself had sat with Gregg while he worked, and Mrs. Casey had been so surprised at his toleration of her there? Yet here he was, allowing Lola to join him. Tanis stood up jerkily, carrying her empty cup.

How, she thought, making for the kitchen, could she get away? The housekeeper thanked her for returning the cup and saucer. Tanis asked, "Is there a telephone booth in the village, Mrs. Casey?"

"There is, Miss Foster, but why bother to walk down there when you could phone from here?" Seeing Tanis's hesitation, the housekeeper added, "If it's private, you don't want to use the hall phone, why not go up to Dr. Barratt's room? There's an extension phone in there. He's busy working and I'm sure he wouldn't mind."

There was, Tanis decided, no way out of that. She entered Gregg's room with a throbbing heart and, wasting no time, dialed Frank Anderson's number. To her relief, he answered at once.

"It's Tanis, Frankie," she said. "There's been some trouble here, and a change of plan. I must talk to you. Is it possible for you to bring the van down here today, later this afternoon, and take me back with you? I'll have a couple of suitcases. Yes, I'm leaving. Have you got room for me at your place? Yes, Cassie's still in hospital. Thanks a lot, Frankie. See you at five-thirty outside the village hall."

"Running into his arms? Is he moving over in his bed to make room for you?"

Tanis swung around. Gregg leaned against the closed door, arms folded, eyes slitted, face unshaven. His shirt was half-open, his slacks creased and fitting closely to his hips. He looked devastatingly, heartbreakingly attractive.

Tanis found she could not answer. Her own heavily

shadowed eyes could not have missed his keen gaze, yet he looked upon her with only derision and condemnation.

"You had to creep up here and call him, did you? You didn't have the courage to use the more public phone downstairs. Why?"

"If you must know—" Tanis lifted her head high "—it was Mrs. Casey who suggested it. You had a visitor. I'm sure she wouldn't have wanted to listen to the conversation of a mere tenant."

"Living here at my expense."

"I said," Tanis returned furiously, "I would pay whatever you asked. I've been in employment until this week, but you just haven't asked. Tell me how much I owe you, for both my keep and Cassandra's, and I'll write you a check."

"You do that, sweetheart. Then you can watch me tear it to shreds."

Just as you've torn me to shreds, she wanted to scream at him, but she choked back the words.

He straightened, pushing his hands into the waistband of his slacks. "I think you've paid me adequately." His eyes skimmed her figure, dwelling indolently on the swell of her breasts beneath the neat blue sleeveless dress. "With kisses, passion, false though it was. You've amused me, helped to fill my leisure hours as a man's *woman* should."

I won't be provoked, Tanis told herself. *I'll take his insults but I won't throw them back. I'll prove, in that way at least, that I'm superior to him.* At the door she confronted him. "Will you please let me pass?"

His arms were folded again. "Give me one good reason why I should."

"Because I hate the very sight of you!" she shrieked, then grew furious with herself for showing him how much his attitude riled her. *So much for my superiority,* she thought bitterly.

His hands shot out and captured her wrists. "I could give a repeat performance of last night and have you on your knees begging me to take you."

"Yes," she choked, "I know you could. But you won't, will you, because your fiancée's downstairs."

"To hell with my fiancée," he snarled, and jerked her against him. Tanis went limp, her head hanging to one side. Slowly his hold on her relaxed. As she had hoped, she had touched the doctor in him. She twisted from his grasp, wrenched open the door and fled along the passage.

The bathroom was a sanctuary. She turned the key and sank to the floor.

CHAPTER ELEVEN

TANIS SAT ON A BENCH outside the village hall eating the sandwiches that Mrs. Casey had insisted on giving her. The housekeeper had been upset at her secret departure, and even more worried about the fact that Tanis had told her she did not require any lunch.

Tanis had waited with hidden impatience while Mrs. Casey made up the sandwiches, anxious that at any moment Gregg might burst in. However, after giving the older woman a note for Cassandra, which she promised to deliver at visiting time that evening, Tanis had exited from Gregg Barratt's home unobserved by him.

It was some time until Frankie's arrival. The day was cloudy but dry, the village street as somnolent as any other village street on a Sunday afternoon. When, half an hour before the specified time, Frankie's van shattered the peace and pulled up in front of her, Tanis was so relieved she almost fell into the passenger seat, leaving her suitcases on the ground.

Frankie got out and stowed them in the van, then returned to the driver's seat. "So glad to see me you can't wait to fling your arms around me?"

Tanis managed a smile. "I like you, Frankie, but not that much!" She sighed. "When we're on our way, and I've recovered some of what's left of my equilibrium, I'll explain."

Frankie nodded, turned the van and they were speeding back to London. By the time they had reached the house that Frankie shared with three friends, Tanis had

told him her story. He had taken Cassandra's final rejection of him with remarkable equanimity.

"Well," he said, remaining in the driver's seat, "since the decorating contract at the Barratt place is off and things have been moving at this end, I'd better let you into the picture." They were parked in the street and other vehicles came and went constantly. He looked at Tanis. "The Foster and Anderson arrangement will have to go."

Tanis made a movement of protest, but he went on, "There have been no more orders from those leaflets. Things are so quiet around here in the decorating line, I got worried. A girl I know—" he gestured toward the house "—she recently moved in—well, her father owns a decorators' supplies store in the high street. He's looking for a manager, preferably someone with experience, who can give expert advice to customers. He's offered me the job. Chrissy, the new girl—that is, his daughter—already works in the shop."

A long sigh escaped from Tanis's throat. She closed her eyes. "So that's that. I'm out of a job, too."

"Sorry, love, but I couldn't turn the chance down, could I? I'd ask if you could work there, too, only I know there isn't a vacancy."

"That's okay," Tanis told him, sounding more confident than she felt. "I'll get a job somewhere. I'll have to, won't I, to pay my share of the rent."

"Talking of that," Frankie commented, his hand poised to open the car door, "when I told you there was room for you, there wasn't, really—at the time. Except sleeping on the floor. But things have developed since then." His grin warned her of what was coming. "Chrissy and I—well, this morning we decided to get together. Now there's her room empty. You can have that. Usual arrangement. Share all facilities, feed yourself. Okay?"

Tanis nodded. So he and the girl Chrissy had got

together. If Cassandra had not turned her attention from Frank to another man, how would she have felt? It seemed not even to have entered Frankie's thoughts.

Chrissy was a pleasant enough girl, the kind of girl Cassandra had been before her accident: full of life and energy, characteristics that had drawn Frank Anderson to her in the first place. Chrissy had cleared her room of her belongings and it did not take Tanis long to settle down. If she appeared to onlookers to be content, it was because she had grown so good at hiding the misery that was eating away at her inner serenity.

The work she found was not to her liking. For a while she worked as a waitress in a café, moving from there to becoming a sales clerk. Both jobs required stamina, and this, she discovered to her dismay, was something she seemed to lack these days. Some mornings she hardly possessed the energy to get to work, let alone stay on her feet for hours at a time.

It was not long before she was joining the crowds who drew unemployment pay. Out of this she paid her rent for her room and bought food and other necessities.

The rent from the two tenants in the house she and Cassandra owned went into a special account at the bank. Half of it was Cassandra's, anyway. Tanis used her share to pay the local taxes and for general maintenance of the property. All of which left her with very little surplus money for items such as clothes.

The whole situation had also drained her of self-respect. Her loss of contact with Cassandra, the nagging pain she felt every time she thought about Gregg, the fear that if she did telephone the house she would discover the Lola's divorce had been finalized and that she was now Gregg Barratt's wife, took its toll of her health and appearance.

One weekend she called on Mrs. Yardley. The woman was delighted to see her, informing her that her friend, the other tenant, was away on holiday. Mrs. Yardley

gave Tanis a cup of tea, told her how ill she was looking and said she needed a few good meals inside her to put a bit of weight on.

Tanis gave a laugh, but it lacked its old ring of happiness and Mrs. Yardley looked at her with pitying eyes. Tanis wanted to tell her that her "illness" was one that no medicine could cure, and that only time would ease it and help her return to her old self. Time, she thought with a sigh, moved very slowly these days.

"Do you think your friend would mind, Mrs. Yardley," Tanis asked, "if I wandered around downstairs for old times' sake?"

"Go ahead, my dear," Mrs. Yardley urged. "Do whatever you want. It's your house."

The room she and Cassandra had shared as a bedroom had changed little except that now only one bed was in use. In a corner stacked away were Cassandra's watercolors. Tanis was delighted to discover that they had been lovingly dusted and were in excellent condition.

Old familiar surroundings gave rise to familiar, well-tried ideas. Having nothing to do, why shouldn't she ask Frankie to take her and the paintings to the roadside tomorrow—she still had the local council's permission to display paintings at that particular place—and make some money that way? Later on, when she had found work that suited her, she would repay Cassandra any money she might earn from the paintings now.

Frankie agreed at once, and next day being Sunday, he drove to the spot and helped Tanis fix the pictures to the railings. There was no sign of her old friend Edna. Maybe, Tanis reasoned, she didn't sell flowers there anymore. Having agreed to pick her up when she contacted him by telephone, Frankie drove away with a wave.

Tanis opened the folding chair she had brought with her, placed the bag containing a flask of coffee and

biscuits beside it and sat down, opening a paperback book. After a while her mind wandered. She thought about Frankie and how well he was doing as manager of the decorators' store. He had told her that it probably wouldn't be long before he and Chrissy were married.

Tanis wondered what the passing weeks had done to Cassandra. There had been a letter from her in reply to her note, saying she was sorry Tanis had not come to say goodbye, but she understood—or had tried to. Tanis had not written in answer to that letter.

Deep down she had not forgiven her sister for wrecking her life—although she acknowledged that it was hardly fair to blame Cassandra entirely. It was her own fault and no one else's, Tanis acknowledged, that she had become so deeply involved with a man she knew to be tentatively engaged to another woman, whom he would marry as soon as she was free.

Spring had become summer, and even that had almost passed. Tanis had scarcely noticed the higher temperatures, the flowers blooming in shop windows, which was the nearest she ever came, in the part of London in which she now lived, to greenery and growing things. Concrete, brick and metal car bodies fleeting past made up the only view that greeted her eyes these days on glancing out of the window.

Now she stared around, breathing the comparatively fresh air, even though it, too, was polluted by passing vehicles. Her eyes rested lovingly on green fields, on the trees in Mrs. Beasley's garden across the busy road, on the birds swooping and perching and flying off again.

Occasionally a car would slow down and the passengers would stare at the pictures on display. Not one, however, stopped at the stand to have a closer look. *Maybe,* she thought, *if I appeared a little more cheerful, smiled encouragingly....* A car slowed down, paused and continued. It did not go far.

Tanis's heart was beating madly. Her heavy eyes

clung to the male figure outlined in the driver's seat, watching, watching to see where the car would go. It turned and drove back along the road, approaching slowly and braking on the shoulder next to her. The paperback book fell to the ground and with shaking hands she retrieved it, pushing it into her food bag.

The driver stayed in the car. He stared at her as she half stood, half sat, uncertainty in every line of her. Why had he come, why didn't he speak, even if only to ask how she was? Or was she imagining it all, as for so many months now she had imagined his face as she lay in her bed, imagined his mouth on hers, daydreamed that his arms were around her?

It was not imagination. The man was moving, getting out, walking toward her. She stood to greet him, her face as unsmiling as his. But there was a difference. Her lack of warmth was due to apprehension and indecision, his to cold contempt. His glance skimmed the pictures.

"How much?" he asked tersely.

"What—what do you mean? Each one, or...?"

"The lot. We've been through this before. Tell me what you want for them all."

She told him how much she was asking for them individually. "There are ten pictures altogether."

He took out his checkbook and jerked his head toward the car. Following him, she told herself she was a fool. She should never trust this man again. Her first sight of him had been right, the first time they had met, here at this same spot.

Then there had been Edna to discuss him with. Now there was only herself and her past knowledge of him. And still her other self obstinately told her this was a man whose integrity she *could* trust, to the ends of the earth.

The interior of the car was so familiar it was like a long-lost friend. Looking at the profile of the owner, who waited, pen poised, before using it, was like con-

templating the jutting corner of a cliff, unscalable and forbidding to dwell upon.

"Do I make this out to you or Cassandra?"

By his harsh tone she knew he had not forgiven her. "To me, please," she answered quietly.

"Why?"

She moistened her lips, thinking longingly of the flask of coffee back in her bag. "I—I need the money. As soon as I can I'll give it back to Cassandra."

"Why do you need the money?"

"I'm unemployed."

He looked at her sharply. "You look half-dead."

"Thank you very much." The sarcasm did not touch him.

He wrote out the check and held it out to her. She looked at the amount. It was, as before, more than the sum she had asked. "That's very kind of you," she said tonelessly. "I won't tear it up, as you threatened to do with any check of mine I might give you. In fact, you can keep it and put it toward what I owe you for Cassandra's and my rent, accommodation and food while living at your house."

A small flare of revenge successfully meted out lighted her eyes but died quickly. He merely put the check loosely back into the book and returned it and the pen to his pocket.

"So Anderson got his sleeping partner in the end." His voice was as toneless as hers.

"Yes, he got his sleeping partner."

His eyelids drooped as he looked her over. "It looks as if you can't keep pace with his sexual appetite. You'll have to warn him to ease off before you collapse, and I do mean collapse."

"Yes," she responded, her voice tight with unexpressed fury, "I'll give him your advice—on medical grounds, of course." Her eyes threw sparks at him like a crackling fire. "You have a textbook knowledge of a

woman's body, haven't you? You told me so yourself."

Gregg stared through the windshield at the massing clouds. "We'd better collect those paintings," he said.

Together they packed the pictures in the back of the car. Gregg folded the chair and put it in the trunk while Tanis placed the bag beside it.

In the car, Tanis said, "Frankie's getting married."

Gregg was as still as the rock he resembled. "To you?"

"To a girl called Chrissy. He's the manager of her father's decorating shop." There was a long pause.

"So—" he turned slowly, contemplating the worn zippered jacket she wore, the jeans that hung on her now that she'd lost so much weight "—he grew tired of you and pushed you out of his bed to make room for another girl."

Tanis did not answer.

"Does it hurt too much to talk about?" he inquired silkily.

She maintained her silence.

Suddenly he started the engine. "I'm taking you home."

Tanis nodded, leaned back and closed her eyes. For the short time she would be in his car—in a quality vehicle like his it would take no time at all to reach London—she decided to make the most of it. There was no doubt that after this she would never see Gregg Barratt again, not after the way she had allowed him to believe the worst of her.

When the car came to a stop she awoke with a start. Her slowly opening eyes showed her that she was still far from London. She turned on him accusingly. "You tricked me. This is where you live, not I!"

"What else did you think I meant? That I'd take you back to some sleazy room in a house where you're plainly completely out of tune with your surroundings, where you've hardly got enough money to feed yourself prop-

erly, and where your ex-boyfriend is living with the girl
he's going to marry? I told you, you look half-dead.
The doctor in me couldn't let you return to that when
the remedy lies in my own hands.''

The doctor in him, she agonized, not the man.... She
challenged, ''So you think living in your house again,
but this time with *your* girlfriend—or is she now your
wife—would make me feel any better?''

Now he chose to remain silent.

Tanis looked around. ''This is Ashdown Forest.''

''You're very astute,'' he returned, quietly sarcastic.
''We're going for a walk.''

''Suppose I choose not to?''

''If you're going to be childish, we'll talk here in the
car.''

After a moment's fight with her rebellious self, she
got out. He followed, locking the car. They made their
way along the rough path into the forest, crackling over
the dry bracken, finding beneath their feet the hard,
dried-out mud of the horse trail, passing through posts
marking the boundaries. The trees were readying themselves for the onset of autumn and there was a distinct
chill in the air.

''Here,'' said Gregg, pulling Tanis down a slope that,
she remembered, led to the hollow in which they had
lain together in the spring. At the hospital in London
from which he must have come, he seemed to have
changed out of the clothes that Tanis had once amusing-
ly looked upon as his working suit. Now he wore a
weatherproof belted jacket and dark slacks. He untied
his tie and opened the neck of his shirt, then pulled off
his jacket, spreading it on the ground.

He indicated that she should sit on the jacket and she
did so, leaving room, expecting him to join her. He
chose instead to sit on the dried bracken. His action hurt
Tanis badly, but she told herself she didn't care.

She pulled off her own jacket, putting it aside.

As casually as possible she asked, "How's Cassandra?"

"In excellent spirits."

"Her legs?" With apprehension she awaited his answer.

"As usual, Russell did an excellent job."

It seemed he refused to give any further information. It could mean that, good job on them or not, Russell Mansfield's work might not have been as successful as had been hoped.

Gregg was half lying back, resting on an elbow. He had picked up a piece of twig and was twisting it. "Start at the beginning," he ordered, breaking the silence, "and carry on until the present moment."

"What's the use?" she answered wearily. "If I tell you the truth you won't believe me now any more than you did in the past."

The twig snapped between his fingers. "Talk, woman."

The massed clouds overhead released a few drops of rain, but they did not seem to worry him. Tanis was scarcely aware of them herself. Part of her objected to his curt manner of speech, the other part acquiesced. "The day I left your house, Frankie took me back to his place. He explained about being offered the manager's job of the decorators' supplies shop. It was the end of Foster and Anderson, he said. Which it was. I tried a few jobs, but somehow I—well, I know it sounds stupid at my age, but I just didn't seem to have enough energy to do them."

Tanis paused. The rain was spattering the surrounding area with large drops, that buried themselves in her hair. Ignoring them, she continued, "I wasn't ill, I was just...." She swung to him. "You should understand. You're a doctor."

"Pining, maybe?"

Had he understood at last? "Yes, yes, I think that's right."

"Couldn't take the rejection."

Did he know now how much she loved him, had missed him? "No, I couldn't, Gregg. When—when you love someone—"

"Couldn't you have moved out, found somewhere else?"

He thought she had been talking about Frankie? She hugged her legs, let her head fall forward, felt drops of rain running down the back of her neck.

"Forget it," she mumbled, wanting to cry, to throw herself on the earth and mingle her tears with the rain, feel the centuries of leaf layers beneath her hands. But she stayed still.

He had moved beside her now. "Forget what?" Her head stayed down. His hand grasped her shoulder and she shivered at the first touch of him for weeks. "Tell me." He shook her. "Forget what?"

"It—it...all of it. The whole damned miserable business." It came now, like the rain that was pouring down. "I wish I'd never met you. I wish you'd never come along that road and found me. We'd still be in my mother's house, Cassie and I. We'd still have our hopes, our dreams, still be saving day by day for her wonder operation that would give her back her youth."

She could not look at him, could not bear to see the pity in his face.

"You had to come into our lives, wreck our peace of mind, show us the better way to live, make us experience it. When all the time it was a dream, a dream that had to end, like all dreams. You, you...." Her head swung toward him, her wet hair lifting. *"You!"*

Her voice was thick, her eyes blurred. She blinked, trying to see him, but the rain had created a premature darkness. A handkerchief wiped her eyes, clearing them, showing her that he was as wet as she was. He was

not smiling. Instead, he was staring at her like a doctor looking at a sick, condemned patient...except that a doctor never looked like that at a patient, because a doctor always had hope in his eyes, never defeat.

There was a look in those amber eyes she could not fathom. Was it defeat? Was it hope? Or was it, worst of all, pity?

He pushed her down with a rough movement, rolled onto her, held her cheeks between the palms of his hands and lowered his mouth. It was the kind of kiss she had dreamed about all those long months, had remembered from past moments when they had entangled and their flesh had touched and there had been a flash, a minor explosion somewhere in mind and body.

She had responded then and she was responding again. He pushed aside her blouse as if he had every right to do so. His hand took possession of the rounded softness beneath. Her body pulsated with desire under his urgent, molding caresses. Her own hands felt the wetness of his shirt and she wanted to touch his skin as he was touching hers.

The trees whispered under the rain's impact and the name Lola drifted into her head. She wrenched her mouth from his and they lay, breathing deeply, staring into each other's eyes.

"What's the use, Gregg?" she asked raggedly. "You're engaged. Or even married now. The game we played—pretending I was your woman—it's over. Why, why did you have to make that condition?"

"Two reasons. I had to do something to keep you away from Anderson."

"You distrusted me that much?" she said, aghast.

"Do you still not understand? I never wanted Frank Anderson. I was so afraid he'd walk out on the business, but worst of all, for Cassandra, I had to stop myself pushing him away each time he touched me. Now do you understand? I kept telling you he wasn't

my kind. In the end he wasn't even Cassie's. She told Dr. Mansfield that Frankie was my boyfriend to let Russell Mansfield know the field was clear for him."

"The scheming little minx! She's never once confessed. The heartache she would have saved if she'd been honest about her tactics. And—" he gripped her chin, depth-testing her eyes "—I believed what she said about you and Anderson."

"That evening you came into my bedroom and savaged me—" her white face grew pink at his smile of reminiscence "—I tried to deny Cassandra's accusations, but you just closed your mind to everything I tried to tell you."

"Woman—" he grabbed a handful of her hair "—I was mad with jealousy. I wanted you for myself. Why do you think I made that proposition, why do you think I made love to you so often if not because I loved you and wanted you—you, above all the women I'd ever known? Do you really think I wouldn't have asked Russell to take over Cassandra's case if you'd refused my demand that you should become my woman?"

"All that time," she accused, "you already had a woman in your life."

"Lola Buxton was never 'in my life.' It pleased her to play around with the idea. She'd been through a bad time with her husband. I let her indulge in her game partly to help her retrieve her self-confidence, and partly to assist me."

"How?" The brown eyes were wide, and in the lightening sky they seemed to be matching the faint struggling rays of the sun. "You don't mean to make me jealous?"

"Perhaps. But most of all, as I said, because I was furious with you—as I thought—your attempts to take Anderson away from Cassandra."

"You never believed me when I denied it."

"Mainly because the visual evidence kept telling me

otherwise. I wanted to hurt you as you, at the time, seemed to be hurting your sister. As you were hurting me." His fingers pressed her chin. "I love you, woman—from the moment I saw you by the side of that road, looking at me with big brown eyes, with such hope that I'd take an interest and maybe buy. I did buy, because of you. I fell so heavily I didn't know what day it was. That was reason two for my making that condition."

"It was the same with me, Gregg, from that first moment. But I thought it was hopeless. There was always Lola—"

"And there was always Anderson. Now they're both out of the way. One's getting married. Right?" Tanis nodded, her eyes holding the sunlight that had fought a battle with the clouds and emerged victorious. "The other has gone back to her husband."

Tanis lifted her head. "The divorce is off?"

"It's off. Lola's reunited with Angus."

Tanis's shining eyes reflected her relief. "Now, please, Gregg—Cassandra?"

"She can walk again."

"She can? She can?" The tears came, held back for so long, no longer tears of unhappiness but undiluted joy.

"She's missed you," Gregg said, lying back, arm behind his head. "When you walk in, she'll weep, too. She'll walk across the room to greet you." A pause as Tanis dried her eyes. "There's something else. Cassandra and Russell are getting married."

"They are? Oh, I'm glad, really glad," Tanis answered. "It's what she wanted. I knew that before I left."

They lay side by side for a long time. Tanis dwelt on the image of Cassandra walking as she used to, laughing and spilling over with life and happiness as she had in the past. Cassandra, an engaged woman.... Even as

she thought about it there was a stab of pain somewhere inside. Cassandra had the love of the man she loved.

"I love you," Gregg had said. But that was all. He didn't need her, as Russell plainly needed Cassandra. He did not—even now—respect her enough to ask her to be his wife, give her his ring, telling the world, "She's mine."

"Tanis—" Gregg's arm reached out, although his eyes were closed "—come to me."

She needed no second bidding, yet she was uncertain how to respond. Kneeling beside him, she touched his cheek. At once arms came out, encircling her, tugging until her body was over his. He held her to him, her cheek on his. His hands felt the shape of her, like an artist lovingly handling a piece of sculpture he had made.

Then he moved quickly, putting her on her back and moving himself onto her again. His hands held her face; he stared into her eyes, then kissed each one. The lean muscularity of his body felt hard and exciting as she strained to mold herself to him.

His lips lowered and lifted all along her lips. "Do you still love me?"

"Oh, Gregg," she answered, her voice wavering, "I love you more now than ever before. You've been with me night and day, in every waking moment, every dream I've dreamed—always, always out of my reach."

He buried his face in her neck. "All those long months, wasted months, without a sight of you. One day I'll tell you what they did to me." He gazed at her again as if he could not fill himself with enough of her. His amber eyes grew darker with desire. "Give me your mouth."

He held her eyes in bondage. Obediently she pouted her lips. "Open them," he insisted. Slowly her lips parted and his came down. She tasted the potent maleness of him, the very essence of the masculinity that was

delving so devastatingly to seek out the very essence of her.

Every part of their bodies that made contact burned and she was consumed by the primeval drive that was flowing out of him and into her.

He said against her lips."If I ordered you to give me your body, would you?"

"Yes, yes," she answered, abandoning her will totally to him now.

He said softly, "I feel for you a love so deep I can find no words to express it. Only actions will do now. I'm going to love you, my darling, my own." He spoke roughly against her throat and a shudder went through her, of wanting and of wanting to give. "I'm going to make you entirely mine. My woman—and my wife."

FREE!
Romance Treasury

A beautifully bound, value-packed, three-in-one volume of romance!

Romance Treasury

An exciting opportunity to collect treasured works of romance! Almost 600 pages of exciting romance reading in each beautifully bound hardcover volume!

You may cancel your subscription whenever you wish! You don't have to buy any minimum number of volumes. Whenever you decide to stop your subscription just drop us a line and we'll cancel all further shipments.